WHITE SMOKE

WHITE SMOKE

NIKHIL MAHAJAN

Srishti
PUBLISHERS & DISTRIBUTORS

SRISHTI PUBLISHERS & DISTRIBUTORS
Registered Office: N-16, C.R. Park
New Delhi – 110 019
Corporate Office: 212A, Peacock Lane
Shahpur Jat, New Delhi – 110 049
editorial@srishtipublishers.com

First published by
Srishti Publishers & Distributors in 2017

*Dedicated to the girl who narrated
this story to me in my dream...*

Acknowledgements

I would like to say thanks to my Bade Papa who strengthened my thoughts and lent his unconditional support; my readers, since they cherished my work and inspired me to keep writing. I owe it to my critics, who are the real friends, a hearty thanks to all who truly make my efforts worthwhile by their constructive criticism.

I would like to thank my sweet li'l girlfriend, who is always in my thoughts as she inspires me to keep writing, and yes, it is because of her that I am a writer today.

Now this is really tough. Although the list is not really long, I have tried my best to acknowledge everyone who has helped me write this novel. I would like to thank my mates Akhil and Shshank for constantly supporting, encouraging and motivating me. Thanks to Amit, Aman, Jai, Pawandeep, Sunil and Varun for being there; they are more like family than just friends.

Thanks Vikram for all the *gyaan*, you have always been a great help. You were the one who guided me towards the right way when I hit a blind end. It was you who gave me the idea of a case study, which lent the story its credible edge.

I'd like to thank my first editor, Bina Biswas, for the book edits – mending it, polishing it and coming up with the best. Aarti Motiani, for the final edits, as she patiently went through the successive first edits and made constructive suggestions along with finalizing the script.

Words would not be enough to describe this special friend Priyanka Dey, for brainstorming this project and giving me new ideas and a vision to write this thriller. I owe my work to Ankita Mahajan, Aniket Kapoor, Gaurav Chawla, Jenny Chawla and Prashant Gandhi.

Thanks to all those who discouraged me, thus in a way strengthening me.

If you wish to know more about me or share your thoughts on the story, do write to me at me@nikhilmahajan.com.

Virat and Payal

The sky was an amalgam of ruby red and orange, highlighting the day end. There was an extensive crowd at the station, but Virat's eyes were fixed on the swollen black clouds that were slowly building up, darkening the sky and blotting out the burning sun. An abrupt shower as the sky opened up, turned the grey black backdrop of the city to light grey and everybody appeared uplifted. Virat tried to mull over the scenario a zillion times, but he could not possibly comprehend the beauty of the whole scene because he was deadened that day and had been suffering a personal crisis. Virat's girlfriend, Payal was not happy with their relationship and was leaving peacefully without giving him even a slightest hint of sadness and pain. This particular gesture of hers irked him. It was the cruelest and the most humiliating moment of his life. They both were like soul-mates. Moreover, she had supported him during his bad times ever since he was fifteen. He did not want to lose her.

"I fear this relationship no longer exists. We seem to be on a balancing rock, watching from either side. The balance is not correct, and so is the relationship. This is like a burden on me, killing me mercilessly with every passing second." Her abrupt negative reply, tinged with a certain amount of cynicism, wasn't ambiguous or even polite in any way.

"I must apologize, but I will now have to leave you to yourself," she added and Virat knew that his life was going to change.

"No, don't… Please don't leave me like this. What would I do, where would I go?" She did not even look at him in the eyes.

"Please…" he pleaded with pain in his heart. But it seemed that she had skirmishes of her own, though nothing as substantial as a deep or meaningful relationship.

With this, they parted ways…

His cries echoed in his mind as he let out another sigh. He was standing on the crowded platform with his bags packed, waiting for the train to arrive. He stood amidst the crowd of unknown faces busy chatting, fighting or simply overlooking all else and hurrying towards their destination. But today, he had to wait. He had to gulp this venom, bear this rough, hard-biting pain deep in his chest. The pain of being left alone.

The train halted and a door slid opened. He stood in front of the open door as people gushed in, pushing him aside as if they were pushing a lifeless entity. After a few seconds, the doors closed and the train started moving again. He stood rooted at the platform. And he realized this world was not fit for him.

She boarded the train a few doors ahead. He saw her, perhaps for the last time, perhaps not. His heart paused at the failing hope, and then he turned around and walked towards the exit.

One day you will realize what you have lost, and when that day comes, you will come running and crying to me, begging on your knees, just like I begged you not to destroy our relationship. But, by then, I will have moved on and will have the guts to break your heart the way you broke mine, he said to himself, the words of self-consolation.

As he reached the other part of the station, he looked at the exit sign, and stood there on the platform. The pain dug deeper inside. The pain of a mangled love. He stood there for a while, not accepting the thought. *The thought of accepting his defeated self, the thought of his defeat against his fight with his pain, the thoughts swirled towards the end unconsciously.* He started walking towards the other end. He waited for another train to pass and suddenly he did what his comatose mind ordered. He compromised his body over his heart. He jumped! The fast moving train crushed his body into a mangled heap.

"Virat, wake up!"

The warden woke him up with a hard twitch. Feeling tired, he slept for a couple of minutes more. He felt worse than he had felt in the dream when he woke up. He glanced at the time, and realized he had only twenty minutes to get to class, which included a ten minutes' walk. He had slept soundly with the dope he had last night and was again late to school like rests of his days. He had suffered a massive psychological damage. Such dreams haunted him every day and he was now used to these terrible nightmares. He was as usual late for class. He huffed, panted, retched, reaching his destination only to find he had misread the tick-tock. It felt like an hour of fretting. Wasting no time and with no interest in attending class, he entered the school building and went towards the hall. It was in the school's curriculum. The teachers were supposed to tell them their marks and give them suggestions that day. Virat entered and took the last seat in the hall. He had made it just in time as his roll number was hardly a few numbers away.

"Why don't you study, Virat? You have failed in your internal exams again," the class teacher shouted in front of everybody with his answer sheets in her hand.

"And the same is repeating again…" the teacher went on mercilessly, and he felt like having been crucified. His body could not take such criticism. He was smitten by this global shame.

"Do you understand? You won't be able to write your final examinations if you do not pass the last internal exam," said the teacher who had turned very unsympathetic towards him as she could see that he was not at all interested in listening to her.

Virat was never a dull student, but he was in extreme pain; a pain that he could not discuss with anyone. He knew that he had no interest studying commerce but his father had forced him hard to study it and then join their family business. He could not disclose his thoughts to anyone, hence he never broke the silence.

"We have to call your father," said his ma'am in front of the whole class as an act of insult. There was nothing in this world Virat would fear more than his father being called for his mistakes. It was not his father's reputation that he wanted to preserve, but he did not want to see him again. He was struck by a thunderbolt as his teacher shouted the final decision.

"You know how much your father loves you? He sent you here in this reputed school, which you do not deserve, just because he wanted to see you rise in your life and be a better person," the teacher continued saying the same thing to every culprit.

"He wants you to study hard and be successful in your life, and look at you… this is how much you respect him!" she kept on scolding him, waving the answer sheets like a fluttering flag in her hand.

"You failed in every semester and this is your final chance, because your board exams are next, and if you fail, trust me, we won't be able to help you," she flatly declared and threw the answer sheets aside roughly.

The hall was empty and the crowd had trooped away. Virat took a chance and went to the staff room to beg the teacher not to call his father, but she was not ready to help him anymore. He knew that he could not convince her, so he went back to class. He could not concentrate anymore as his teacher's words kept haunting him, hurling him back into the past.

A few years back…

Virat was quite aware of the long, lonely nights that awaited him. He knew that his conscience would be burdened by the silence about the known betrayal and disloyalty of his father too. No matter how brilliant their world looked from outside, it would not lighten their numb lives. His father was mostly out for business and the only son, the product of their unfortunate and unsuccessful marriage, had always been short of love and given the responsibility of his sick mother. The ambience at home had kept him away from people and his social life was almost non-existent.

"Virat, can you please go and pick up your father from his office?" Virat's mother was in bed and his father was late.

She was vexed. He knew his mother would not have her food before his father came back, but the medicines were a priority as well. She was on her death bed and was suffering from cancer; these were the last days of her life. Her lungs were contracting, the mucous formation was thick. Her wind pipe constricted, and chemotherapy had made her lean with a low immune system. She huffed every two hours for which she needed a bronchodilator pump and sometimes a nebulizer session. It was a numb home, a home devoid of warmth, a home staring at death. There was no treatment since this was the final stage of cancer.

Virat left home to search for his father as he was also concerned. He went to his father's office building; it was all dark and damp since it was late in the evening. He reached the upper floor where he could see a light seeping through the door. The door of the office creaked opened and he flung into total darkness, a big black hole of nothingness. As he reached a little closer to the main office, he heard a sigh followed by a sickly temperate moan, then sighs followed by the sticky dull guttural 'ahs'. A faint shadow was moving. Did he see it right? Two bodies? The image he saw was dark. It was not clear, but evident a female form was on the top of a man he could hardly identify. But he understood that the two people in that room were making love. He tried to identify the people in the act, but nothing was clearly visible. The lady was moving faster with each stroke, enjoying the strength of the man she was being banged by on the office table. He kept on looking at the act, their passion and pain for each other. It was too much for an innocent heart to find two adult giving vent to their needs. Testosterone gushed through Virat's body as he had never seen something like this. Hands rubbing over each other, body over body as they savoured every moment. The hazy scene left Virat confused.

Suddenly Virat came closer, and he could see their faces in the faint light. He could not believe what he saw. He saw his father in the act of sin. He decided to stay a little longer, but suddenly Virat's dad turned to a new position and saw him. Despite that, he shamelessly continued fucking his secretary. Virat left the place in a daze. The whole moment got buried inside his innocent heart. He could not believe what his father was up to when his mother was on her death bed. Nobody discussed what happened and they both stopped talking to each other. The hatred and pain got buried deep inside Virat's heart.

That year, Virat's mother died, and he was eventually sent to a boarding school in Shimla. But the pain and the thoughts never left Virat's mind and kept haunting him. An innocent mind was thus polluted.

"Why don't you study hard?" Karan tried to console Virat, and suddenly he came back to his senses. Karan was the only friend Virat had.

"I will try." He said nothing more. Then Karan left the class as Virat sat there unaccompanied, calming himself down.

He still remembered…

While his father remained uncaring towards his mother who was dying of cancer, he had been strong for her. But the day his mother passed away peacefully in her sleep, Virat broke down. The memory was still fresh in Virat's mind. It was a hollow pain. While he was sent off by his father to the Shimla boarding school, he probably expected him to be there, holding his hand. His mother had always taken care of him. But now, there wouldn't be anyone asking him to grab a bite before he left home or offer him a hot meal when he came back. Virat knew the world was going to be tough for him. He knew that there was one more reason why his father had sent him away – his father's slimy affair with his secretary.

He sighed as he reached the hostel. He unlocked the door and remembered his mother's face during their last meeting when she had been well, and her sweet, humming, and warm embrace.

"You were right Maa, I never grew up." Virat cried hard, shedding tears of pain on his pillow.

"I wish I never grew up, for I remember being everything, everything else except your little son. Will you ever forgive me?" he lay on his bed, crying yet another time.

"She will, I think, she had a golden heart... a mother's heart..."

Virat had no choice but to live at the boarding where he had been sent. Books became his world since then. And in between this, he found his true love Payal and a friend Karan who really cared for him. Despite the comfort he found in their company, they were not so close to him that he could share his pain with them. Virat felt he was all alone and could not even work with his friends. He actually had no friends. Virat was all alone in the big world; all alone in the crowd.

▼

Mahi and Arjun: Love at first sight

Arjun was the only son of a Bengali mother and a Gujarati father, who was also a business tycoon. He was an incredibly good-looking guy with an easy childhood and a stable life. He was the richest chap in school; his father was a millionaire-businessman who lived in Delhi. Spending time with his Dad also included a trip to New York to meet his mother. His father, who remarried, had a second wife who lived with them but had no kids. To make his life worse, he was once in a long distance relationship, but then due to his addiction to drugs, that relationship did not last long.

"Hey girls, leave the place in five seconds!" shouted Arjun as he entered the girls' toilet on the second floor of the school.

He was dressed in a crisp white shirt and blue school pants and seemed to be drenched in deodorant. His masculine edges rounded off from his shirt, and one could imagine the broad chest beneath it.

All the girls ran towards the door to leave the place. Every girl was afraid of Arjun when he was high. This was his favourite place. He placed a book on the shelf there and asked Eshaan, his close friend for the drug LSD, "Fast, we have just two minutes."

Eshaan wasted no time and pulled out the secret packet and threw it in front on him. They smiled at each other. Then Arjun placed the powder on the book, pressed it hard to check the mixture, and then he took a thousand rupee currency stiff note, and rolled it like a straw. He snorted at it hard with his nose and swilled, closing his eyes.

"This is real, wow this is it!" His eyes turned red within seconds. It was Eshaan's turn next. And then again the straw was handed back to Arjun and he bent over making room to snort the drug.

Suddenly, a girl opened the door and entered. She was a new girl; tall with a fine pair of shoulders having the forthright honesty of a child. Plus, she had this really positive attitude and an incredibly beautiful face. Wearing the school blazer, she made her way towards the sink, or rather she took one step to her right, where the doors had been removed, to allow a shelf beneath to which a counter was mounted with a wash basin on top.

"Holy fuck!" she screamed aloud as she looked at the sight.

Since she was the new girl in the school, she did not know that no one else in the school had the fortitude to enter the place where Arjun stood.

Eshaan looked at her and shouted in anger, "Out, you bitch!"

But she wasn't like the other girls in the school and screamed back, "What the hell? Mind your language. You are in the girls' toilet!"

This was the first time Arjun had heard someone yelling at him, so he smiled.

"You don't know me?" he tried to introduce himself as he moved towards her slowly.

"Some rich dad's boy with poor etiquettes?"

She was already told about these boys, so she gave a wicked smile which was really disappointing for a stud like him.

"Do you want me to make a video of you on my mobile?" Mahi retaliated taking out her mobile from her pocket.

"Let me get hold of you." Eshaan moved fast.

"Stop!" Arjun stopped Eshaan showing his hand.

"Come in and pee."

He knew she was there to pee, so pointed towards one of the cabins.

"Bastard!" she yelled again in anger.

Arjun heard her and that made him angry. He held her hand and shoved her towards the wall, putting his hand on hers and pressing it hard.

"Ah!" the girl cried in pain. He then grabbed Mahi's wrist, rolled her and got hold of her in his arms. Arjun's face was now close to hers and they both could smell and hear each other's breath. Mahi's heart pounded fast. She was scared.

Arjun had never felt anything for anyone, but that day, it was different. He wanted to interact with her, and he just started saying, "I like your guts, the way you retaliated."

She turned her face away, but he continued softly. "What's your name, sweetie?" Mahi kept silent for a few seconds.

She never lacked courage; she wriggled the sleek thing out of her jeans' back pocket. With beguiling eyes she caught his attention, while with a jerk she pulled her right hand and set it free.

The spray hit Arjun's eyes and he was in extreme pain. The grip was lost. Eshaan ran to rescue him, but he was too late. Before he could do anything, Mahi quickly sprayed the pepper spray into his eyes too, but he managed to hold her wrist.

"Fuck! Look out for that!" Arjun screamed to warn Eshaan.

"My eyes are burning!" Eshaan cried loosening his hold. Mahi sprayed the pepper spray on Arjun again, just to be doubly sure.

Both of them were now on the floor, rolling in pain. Arjun could hear the girl's steps heading out. Inching towards the door, Mahi fumbled to get to the knob of the door. All fingers and thumbs, luckily the door opened and she almost exited.

"Tell me your name at least!" Arjun screamed in pain, rubbing his eyes.

"Mahi," she uttered her name, stomped out and let the door slam shut.

"I think I like her," Arjun smiled. The effect of the dope seemed to have waned out with the spray.

Arjun was a rich dad's boy. Every morning, he had to choose between his Gucci and Armani school blazers. He was the only guy who drove his own car to school and on the way, he'd pick up his friend, Eshaan, another rich dad's boy. They weren't interested in studies, and rather liked disturbing everyone. They had a group called V3. Eshaan was also an active member of V3 and the third sleeping partner of the group was the son of an Italian businessman whose father worked with the embassy and was active in Indian government politics.

One day...

Things weren't getting any better after his mother's departure. It was time for Virat to return to pick up the pieces of his life. He decided to party. Virat, along with Karan and some other friends, gathered for the feast. Their venue was a grand house. The furniture in the house was covered with plastic and they were instructed to take care of it. There were collectable porcelain vases kept everywhere, which looked expensive and rare.

The party went well and it was late. Most of the guests had left. A glut of emotions swept through Virat, bowled him over. He was on a mission, and he had something to prove to himself. He hit upon an idea. He decided to get intimate with his girlfriend Payal and shared this thoughts with Karan.

"Virat, are you really going to get physical with her? Do you think it is right to do such a thing in a public place?" Karan asked Virat.

"Yes," he laughed it away.

"Okay, meet you back at the parking when you are done," said Karan patting Virat's back.

"Will meet you later at the backyard of the hostel," Virat informed Karan with a smile. A couple of hours later, after enjoying the requisite fag, he called Payal.

"We will make out in the forest, what say?" he confirmed his plan. They already had shared this idea, but Payal was still confused about making it happen.

"No, please Virat, this isn't safe," Payal replied.

"C'mon, trust me," he pleaded.

"I don't find it safe being a girl," she again replied angrily.

"Meet me first, we will see about it on the way."

"Okay." Virat was so convincing that Payal could not refuse. Every time a little pressure from his side to persuade her worked well.

For safety, he parked his car outside the girl's hostel and Payal went inside to assure her presence and she stood there in the hostel with her mates for a while so that no one would notice her missing later on. After ten minutes, Virat called her and she moved towards the hostel gate secretly. It was now decided. A date; a night out in the woods.

Her room was on the fifth floor of that old-fashioned hostel. These rooms were equipped with an old fashioned toilet basin, portable electric grills, a bed, one small battered chair and a plastic wardrobe. The girls had this habit of keeping their doors open so that they could converse without leaving their rooms. There were a number of small rooms on the ground floor too where the staff used to live. It was difficult for Payal to leave the hostel. But at that moment, no one seemed to be around and she managed to escape. After a little while, Payal came in sight while she crossed the road and Virat quickly moved towards the decided place as it was not safe for him to wait for her outside the hostel.

It was a dark cold night. Payal watched the street lights flicker down the street. The cicadas sang full songs as she walked through the couple of short blocks to meet him away from her hostel.

Wearing high heels of cherry red color with a matching handbag, a short fitted black dress draping over one tanned shoulder while exposing the other, her long dark brown hair was pulled up into a playful pony tail. She felt warm and carefree as she approached the decided place to meet him. She saw him standing in front of the bus stop, preoccupied with his phone.

Virat looked relaxed in his light blue chinos and white t-shirt. *He has been getting some sun, his nice golden tan on those bulging biceps,* she thought while she looked up and went near him.

"You look gorgeous," he said as he wrapped his arm around her waist and they leaned in for a quick hello kiss before he escorted her to the car. She looked so pretty that Virat could never imagine someone being so beautiful. As she came close and looked into his eyes, Virat looked back romantically. He noticed she was wearing lenses.

"Are you wearing lenses? Your eyes look pretty when they are hazel," he said.

"Yeah!" Payal replied. She leaned back, resting her head on the back of the seat so her chin tilted upwards. He thought how beautiful she was! Driving a little out of the city, Virat offered her his hand, which she held after turning on the radio. After fiddling with the station control, she tuned into a dance band. Turning the volume up, she leaned back, tapping her foot in tune with the music.

For the first time during that month, there was rain, which fell steadily on the parched ground, releasing an arousing smell of dampness that pleased Payal. Virat could not believe that finally they were going to make out. As decided a day before, they parked in the woods so that no one could see them.

"It's alright here." His voice was warm and reassuring.

"You want this?" She cooed and led him on, "Be brave and like a good little slave, give me everything." Virat smiled. He came upon Payal like an ambitious bee that sees an exotic flower that must be milked for honey. With a sigh of pleasure that was almost a sob, she surrendered and he slid his fingers all the way inside.

"You feel unbelievably wet and so sexy," he said as he slowly, gently fucked her with one finger, all the while stretching her just a little until she moaned with lust.

Her whole body was trembling now, "Oh! Please, please, I need to come, I want to come," she almost sobbed.

Her wanton lust was so powerful that he could feel it radiating through her in waves, but he had not finished yet. Withdrawing his finger, he took hold of the seat clamp and plugged it to lean it down, making it a bed. The space was neither too small, nor too big, but just right to perform. He smeared it with lube and then slid in, easily. But when it reached its widest point, he needed to give his time for his muscles to cope with this new sensation.

"Oh... Oh...!" she mewled like a kitten, incoherent, with pleasure and the desperate desire of release.

"Oh yes! Fuck yes...!" She cried as the butt plug slipped in and his muscles clamped tight around the narrow base and held it firmly in place.

He reached around to slowly stroke her clitoris and give it a sharp smack and then a gentle caress.

"Oh... God yes...!" She screamed as Virat slid into her with more gush.

She had never felt so complete, so completely possessed. Her whole body shook with uncontrollable desire – she had never felt so vulnerable, so beautiful, so desired, and so completely free. Staring down at each other, they could feel the roar of her orgasm building like a tsunami. Finally they both reached the highest peak, pumping harder into her Payal whispered in his ear: "I am coming and I wish you to come with me now!"

Screaming, writhing, shaking, sobbing, she came with juices and the waves of ecstasy. Slowly their bodies subsided – warm, soft and sleepy. Wasting no more time, they started to wear their clothes. Payal went out to pee and Virat waited for her in the car.

After waiting for about five minutes, he felt he should go out and look for her. It had been a while and they had worked themselves out; he wanted to check if she had fainted. He went out in search of her.

Suddenly he saw a lady with blood all over her face in the shadows. Petrified, Virat got back into the car. He sat waiting, his heart thumping hard against his chest. Was the face real or had he imagined it?

"Why are you so scared?" Payal was back in the car.

"Nothing," Virat replied huffing. After all, he did not want to scare her.

"Let's drive away."

The rain had ceased, but the roads were slippery and glistened in the headlights. He drove carefully. After driving a little distance, he heard a very faint squeak. He could not do anything other than give pace to the car. He looked at the girl sitting by his side, who he had made out with a minute ago.

"Did not you hear a strange noise?" he asked.

"No," she replied.

A pause prevailed; this continued for a few seconds until he decided that he had no choice but to drive back to the hostel rather than go to the party. Suddenly, while turning the car abruptly, Virat hit a girl. This scared the hell out of him and utter confusion ensued. He needed to control the car to save themselves, and hit a tree with a thud in the same bid. He rested there for a minute. When he had caught his breath and was slightly calmed, he looked up and saw bodies hanging from the tree he had hit.

He looked at Payal for reassurance, but her head had hit hard on the dashboard and she was bleeding. She lay there unconscious. He opened the door of the car to get a grip of the situation. He came closer to see and realized that one of the dead bodies hanging from the tree looked like him. He froze for a moment. He quickly ran back towards the car.

And just like that, with a heavy heart and tears in his eyes, he woke up from his dream. Virat had always admitted to the feeling of being trapped in the wrong body. He could relate. There were times when he felt trapped in the wrong life, but he wasn't going to slit his wrists or end this pain. He lay down for a minute with his heavy heart pounding from the fear of the recent nightmare and closed his eyes.

"Hey, you are late for the school again." The warden gave a blow of the stick to Virat.

He was again late for the school. Such weird dreams were now more frequent. Virat knew his mental health was deteriorating day by day. He had to trust someone to share these things with, someone who rather than making fun of him would try and help him look for a solution.

Virat and Payal
Another day at school

This was a time when the relationship between Payal and Virat was at stake. Virat always used to dream about them making out and most of the times the dreams would break up with a weird finale. He was confused about this relation. Payal was now a liability and nothing else. Since Virat was caught up with so many other thoughts, he could not concentrate on his studies. Karan suggested he should visit the library.

Virat was dejected with this girl. He could envision her as a vampire; he knew he had no way out. He always liked her as an innocent girl, but now his thoughts had altered. She never rescued him from his tribulations; she rather became a problem herself. He had no friends other than this girl. They had been together for the past two years, ever since Virat had joined school. But now Virat had changed as he faced the nightmares. He could not carry on with this relationship. They seemed to be just dragging it out.

"Are you listening?" Payal again screamed after he had ignored her for the umpteenth time. She craved for his love and care. She screamed at him again and left the library.

His love for books and his belief that books actually let him live a separate life apart from the one of his own, had made him become friends with the books ever since he had changed school. For him, these books were humans in every way.

Virat had nothing to do; he searched for a book to read. Unfortunately for him, he picked a novel titled *An Unpublished Story* which was going to change his life forever. He read the blurb which gave him no clue of the story. As he went through a few pages of the book, while flipping through the pages he saw a passport sized picture of a beautiful girl tucked between the pages.

She looked tall, stunningly-thin with thick-dye-flaxen-hair that reached her shoulders. Her skin was milky-white, her mouth was wide and beautiful coral eyes complimented her looks. She wore a green turtle-necked sweater which had not been in fashion since a few years, but still looked fresh on her. Her looks were soft. Her high cheek bones gave a soothing effect to her face. He looked at the picture closely to check the identity of the girl.

"What a beauty," he said to himself as he held the picture closely. He looked at it for a few seconds without blinking even once, and then put the picture back inside where he had found it and kept the book aside.

But this picture had something mysterious in it which made Virat look at it once again. He opened the book again, flipped through the pages and took the picture out. This girl in the picture was beautiful, but she had never been seen in the school.

I should know you, he thought.

Virat knew almost every girl that age in school, but had never seen her, so his curiosity took over. He took the picture along with him in his pocket and went back to the hostel. On the way back, he saw Payal passing by. He hid himself behind one of the pillars and she passed by without noticing him.

"Did you see her?" he asked the picture.

"She is my girlfriend," he continued.

"You should have been my girlfriend in her place," he complained to the picture, but more to himself.

Well you must have been a very beautiful girl during your times, and how could someone leave your picture inside that book... I would have never done so, it would have been very close to my heart, he thought.

As he reached his room, he felt very tired. He threw his rucksack down and changed his clothes. He switched on the bathroom lights. Preparing his bed to sleep, he kept the picture on the study table and lay down to sleep.

▼

CASE NO 242

Mathur had many enemies. Until the moment he fell into disgrace, he had always treated his seniors with cold contempt. Many of his seniors had asked for him be transferred to Delhi, pointing that he could be used behind the scenes, and they could make him a trusted clerk. Hence, Mathur was sent to Delhi and loaded with routine and dull paper work. There was nothing he could do except hate his dishonest seniors. He never accepted this fact that he was no longer the best and had been removed from the active field and given a desk job, until he was given this last chance to prove himself.

On this brilliantly sunny August morning, Delhi was at its best. From his large window, Mathur, the head of the Delhi Division, who also served State police Intelligence, relaxed in his executive chair, contemplating the view through the window with a benign smile. His cabin was medium-sized but very functional. All kind of electronic paraphernalia lay on the desk. A small camera was mounted over the desktop. There was also an iPad, scanner and a printer. Mathur was notoriously fastidious about hygiene. With thirteen years of service behind him, he had a good reason to be the best officer the department had. The office telephone was like a bane of his life. One moment he had peace and it was quiet; the next moment the telephone would shatter the atmosphere.

Lifting the receiver, he said, "Yes?" and the bad news came in. He was told to dedicate his lovely August monsoon to the new murder in the capital which was in the news these days. Bhandey, his assistant, handed over the case report to him.

Sub Divisional Police Office Daryaganj.
SR-A Police Station Daryaganj District Central Delhi.

Subject: - Inquest proceedings U/S 174/Crpc into the death of Rishi Singhal and family S/o J.D. Singhal R/O Daryaganj Tehsil Central Delhi
District Central Delhi, initiated vide DDR No.06 dated 05-04-2015, P/S Daryaganj.

1.	Name of the person who lodged the report	: Police Station Daryaganj.
2.	Date of occurrence.	: 05-04-2015.
3.	Date of report and time	: 05-04-2015.
4.	Name of the deceased with full particulars	: Rishi Singhal s/o J.D. Singhal; J.D. Singhal s/o S.S. Singhal; Anu Singhal w/o J.D. Singhal; r/o Central Delhi.
5.	Name of the persons who dentified the dead body	: Shankar r/o BodalGarh, Bihar (Servant).
6.	Apparent cause of death	: Suicide case.
7.	Place from where the dead body was recovered	: Central Delhi.
8.	Age & Sex	: 2 - Male; 1 - Female
9.	Injuries found on the dead body	: No Injuries found on any of the bodies.
10.	Name of the I/O	: ASI Mustaq Ahmed.
11.	Name of the office Incharge of P/S	: Inpst. Paramjeet Singh SHO P/S Daryaganj.
12.	Name of the supervisory officer	: Dy.SP. Dewakar Singh, SDPO Daryaganj.

Brief facts of the inquest proceedings are that on 05-04-2015, an information was received at P/S Daryaganj through reliable source to the effect that dead body of Rishi Singhal, s/o J.D. Singhal; J.D. Singhal, s/o S.S. Singhal, Anu Singhal w/o J.D. Singhal, r/o Daryaganj were found dead at their residence. Since the death of deceased has occurred under suspicious circumstances and to ascertain the cause of death nothing can be said until the medical reports come. Inquest proceedings U/S 174/Crpc has been initiated vide DDR No.04 dated 22-04-2015 at Police Station Daryaganj. The enquiries entrusted to ASI Mustaq Ahmed of Police Station Daryaganj.

Hence SR-A is submitted.

NO: 242/SDR
Dated: 23/Aug/2015

**Dy. Supdt. of Police,
SDPO Daryaganj**

Copy to:
1. Inspr.Genl.of Police JZ Daryaganj
2. Inspr.Genl.of Police C&R Daryaganj
3. Dy.Inspr.Genl.of Police ND Range Central Delhi
4. Sr.Supdt.of Police Daryaganj
5. Supdt.of Police Hqrs. Daryaganj
   .... for favour of kind information please.
6. SHO P/S Daryaganj for information and necessary action.

SDPO Daryaganj

Looking at the photocopy of the case report submitted by the Investigating Officer, Mathur smiled for the justice they did to the investigation. The case report was way below his expectations; the report was made under inquest reporting which means it was all a mess with no clues. Mathur was a man who hardly had faith in the investigation done by the police department, so he decided to look at the case briefly. He was one of the best agents in the country, but due to the interference of politicians in matters of law and order, honest officers like him were drawn back to the concrete walls. He looked as though he had shrunk with age. A slightly aged man in a dark grey suit, with silver hair and watery eyes that sank back into his face. He looked so tired as though he had not slept for days. This was an unassailable proof that his work had been and was still beyond reproach and that he could consider himself indispensable.

"I need more details on this case," said Mathur to the other fellow agent. "I don't consider this a case of suicide," he continued with a grin on his face.

"Think, why would a millionaire poison himself? Or his family? What kind of crisis he might be going through?" he added a suspicious note to the case.

"This is a unique case." He bent a little looking at the photographs carefully.

"There is no sign of injury, nor were they so immature to have poisoned themselves." He opened his drawer and took out his magnifying glass to have a look at the photographs.

"What do you think, Bhandey?" Mathur asked for a second opinion. Bhandey was his associate. Though he was not very honest, but he made a good partner with Mathur. His chest hair met with his beard line, which went all the way upto his forehead and made him look like a B-grade Bollywood villain.

"I need details of all the suspected people who dealt with him and that his company dealt with!" Mathur ordered him as he could smell something suspicious in the entire affair.

Another fellow officer entered his cabin. He sat down to listen.

"I need to enter their residence to solve this mystery, if you allow me, as the police department has sealed it," Mathur asked his fellow officer.

"I will ask my senior regarding this," he replied to Mathur who waited eagerly to start his investigation with a new angle and left.

He then took hold of the second case sheet submitted to him by the police department:

Sub Divisional Police Office Daryaganj.
Sho P/S Daryaganj.

Subject: - Minutes of Crime review meeting of P/S Daryaganj held in the P/S Daryaganj on 23-05-2015.

Please refer to Supdt. of Police Hqrs. Central Delhi's office letter No.666-64/Rdr/12/SPHQJ dated 24-05-2015, regarding the subject cited above. You are hereby directed to submit the follow up action taken report to the concerned quarters under intimation to this office.

NO: - /SDR   Dated: - /2015

**Dy. Supdt. of Police,
SDPO Daryaganj**

Copy to:
1. Supdt. of Police Hqrs. Central Delhi for favour of kind information please.
     This is in reference to his office letter no. and dated quoted above.

SDPO Daryaganj.

Mathur knew there was still room for some more investigation and the case sheet also referred to the same. The door opened, a senior officer along with Bhandey peered into the office. The officer looked young, tough, good-looking, yet dangerous. The senior officer took a seat whereas Bhandey stood by.

"Sir, he is working on case 242," Bhandey introduced Mathur, and they shook hands later.

"What do you have to say about the case?" the senior asked impatiently.

"I think we need a little more in-depth investigation," Mathur replied.

"Well, then I have a clue for you." He handed him a photograph of the crime scene. Mathur took the envelope and kept it on his table. The senior stood up, put his hand in his pocket, took a cigarette, lit it, took a puff and let the smoke drift down his nostrils.

"It's never a waste of time. Where there is a will, there is a way," he said and walked out of the office, leaving a photograph on Mathur's table.

Mathur took out a table lens to have a keen look over the photographs. There were no revealing clues that he could see in the first go, but the bluish nails were one of the hints that the officer might have noticed and had hidden intentionally to end this investigation since it was a high prolific murder case. Mathur was sure that such a bluish color on the nails and other distinct parts of the body is always due to less flow of blood in the body. It certainly seemed like hard metal poisoning. He knew something had been taken orally or injected, but which drug was used had to be found out. He also knew that the hard metals are amongst those few products one cannot get without a prescription or which could only be obtained from a laboratory. And this was another hint. Mathur picked up his phone.

"Connect me to the officer in charge in the Pathology and Finger Print Bureau, Miss Daisy," he ordered his assistant and in a minute he was on the line with a pathologist. Mathur pressed the bell to call Bhandey to his desk while Daisy came on the line.

"Hello, this is Inspector Mathur speaking," he introduced himself.

"Yes sir, reporting," Daisy greeted.

"I want the report of the drug which has been used in case 242," Mathur asked for the report.

"I have not yet received any kind of pathological review for the case, sir," she replied.

"Let me do the paperwork from my office and get you in touch with the case and the samples."

"I hope the samples have been taken in a serious manner and no violation while collecting the sample has been committed," she feared about the sample handling. "It will take a week to do a culture test for every sample. I will submit the report within five days after I receive the samples."

"Fine, I will connect with you within the next twenty-four hours for acknowledging further progress," Mathur continued.

"Daisy will be in connection with you, Bhandey," Mathur handed over the matter to his assistant.

Mathur was one of the finest officers in the department. Case 242 was a suicide case, one of the biggest mysteries the city had seen. This case had a political involvement as the family was one of the richest in the country, while their son was allegedly under trial in court for raping a minor. In the first go, this case looked like a case of revenge, but this was a second level murder case. The attack was brutal because not even a single person from the family was spared.

The phone rang. "Hello, Inspector Mathur," he answered.

Someone called his name in a single tone. "How are you handling the case, Mathur? We have deployed you for results, we need no more shame," said the IG from the other side.

"Sir, I can give results, but I need to have some investigation power to examine this case without any interference," Mathur shielded himself as he knew the case was politically so strong that a few people in the society would not be happy about Mathur working on it.

"I need no violation, this case is already in the news. You can go out in a de-novo way, solve it in your own way. Just that I don't want you taking any help from the CID officers. They are already working on this case. I want our department to solve this case independently," he continued.

"Yes sir!" he said as he disconnected the line.

Virat and Payal

Next morning, when Virat woke up distracted by the sunlight, he felt fresh as never before. The trees were glittering with their fresh green foliage. Spring had sprang upon the world and flowers peeped shyly out of the hard soil. There seemed to be a universal sigh of relief. He opened the drawer of the bedside table and checked for the picture. It was still with him. He looked at it and smiled as if he had some kind of connection with it.

"Hello!" he greeted the girl in the picture with a smirk; he had forgotten the fact that the previous night he had kept the picture on the study table carelessly. He didn't think much on how it had landed there in the drawer in the morning.

He took the picture along with him and went to the bathroom. He fixed it on the mirror and brushed his teeth. A million thoughts kept coming in his mind. While brushing his teeth, he constantly kept thinking – what would be the name of this girl? If she was his classmate, would he have proposed to her? Then he went for a bath and quickly got ready for breakfast in the school mess. On the way to the mess, he was greeted by the boy who served the students in the mess. Virat had never visited the mess so early. Mostly he used to miss his breakfast.

"What's on the menu today?" Virat asked.

"Today we are serving South Indian dishes," the boy replied.

"An omelette," he ordered as he was uninterested in South Indian food.

"Today is Tuesday sir!" the boy reminded him.

"I want two omelettes with onions and tomatoes," he said in a bossy manner. Virat was always very stiff if anyone suggested something. This was ingrained in his personality because of all the negativity he had in himself due to the tribulations in his life.

Before his breakfast could be served on the table, suddenly Virat looked for the picture in his pocket but remembered he had forgotten it in the bathroom over the mirror. And as soon as he remembered his last talk with it, he wasted no time and hurriedly ran straight to his bathroom. To his utter surprise, it wasn't there. He was very confident about where he had left the picture last, but it was not there. He again searched for it in his clothes, but he could find nothing. He knew he had lost it.

After losing the picture of the girl, he felt very annoyed. It was not there, but it had to be somewhere. In rage, he kicked the bucket hard for this loss. He knew if someone had taken it, then he would never get it back. He felt helpless and wondered why he had become so attached to that picture. He felt restless and went into his room again for the final search.

Finally, losing all hope, he lay on the bed to recover from the loss. And just as unexpectedly, he found the picture lying on the floor. He wondered when he had thrown the picture there. But it was with him, and he was relieved.

"Hey friend, you missed me?" he talked to the picture. "Come on, I am back now," he kissed the picture and kept it in his pocket with care.

He was again late for class, and he knew he would be scolded.

"Happy birthday!" shouted everyone at once when he entered the class.

Virat was surprised. Amidst all his nightmares and his newfound friend in the picture, he had completely forgotten that it was his birthday.

"Here are the sweets," the class teacher handed a packet to him. "Your father sent it through courier a few days back," she continued.

It was the first time Virat was not angry at his father. Instead, he was happy that at least one day from the rest of the year he had not been scolded for being late.

"Thank you," he whispered to the picture in his pocket.

"You saved me," he continued as if the girl in the picture had saved him and imagined that she wished him. Yet another incident happened, and Virat was now more confident about his life. He believed the picture had changed his destiny and his luck.

Arjun and Mahi

The sun rose from behind the hills, first lighting the top of the trees. He had never before noticed the beautiful mornings. Arjun's beard had been shaved by his valet, and he was now putting his white and crimson school t-shirt, and on his thin, bronze wrist was a gold bracelet that held a gold Omega watch in position as he paced the vast floor of his bedroom. The May air was sharp but pleasant. The first rays of the sun entered the room, lightening the rich color of the walls and the splendid Persian carpet on the floor. The comfortably furnished room was untidy with a number of empty gin and whisky bottles lined up along the windowsill.

His breakfast lay on the trolley, which was parked in the centre of the room. Silver foil kept the dishes warm. He considered it to be the most important meal of the day. He went to the trolley and lifted the first and then the other silver cover. Scrambled eggs was his favourite breakfast meal. But he did not feel too hungry for it. He skipped the main meal, grabbed a slice of buttered toast and left for school. He had something very important to talk about.

"Hi!" Arjun tried to stop Mahi. "Sorry for that day," he continued.

"You think you are cool enough to impress me?" she asked.

"I think nobody matches you here like I do," he beamed.

"Like what?" she asked.

"Gucci and Prada!" He tried to impress her with his as usual assets.

"Who cares about what you wear." She gave him a cold shoulder. "And what about manners?" She started moving towards the parking.

It was again an insult to Arjun. He followed her fast, as she took a turn towards the back of the building. "Listen when I am talking to you."

Mahi gave no reply and kept walking. Arjun decided to retaliate, because he wasn't used to such behaviour from others. So he came from the back and putting his hand around her waist, lifted her with his muscular arms. Passionately, he threw her towards the wall. While holding her hands in his, giving her no chance to escape as he knew she was a clever girl, he quickly kissed her lips.

"I can have anything I want," he looked into her eyes and gave her a tender kiss on her lips again.

"I am just giving you a chance to like me. I want you to feel the same way I feel for you. Don't take me that lightly," Arjun said to Mahi, but she looked away.

"I told you I like you, and whatever I like, I get it, by hook or by crook," he said and released her.

She wriggled free and tried to move away, when Arjun stopped her and said, "A girl like you is meant to be loved."

It was like an insult to Mahi; a tear rolled down from her eyes as she had never been humiliated like this. He just did what he had in his mind, but she could not get over the fact that she had been forcibly kissed by Arjun publically and molested by him so roughly. While Arjun walked towards his car commandingly, happy over his act, she remained silent for a while.

"Happy now?" asked Eshaan, who was already sitting in the car. He knew about Arjun's plan and was waiting in the car.

And then something happened that nobody could have imagined.

Arjun turned the keys of the car, and before he could race it, suddenly a car appeared from behind. Arjun could only hear the humming sound because of the speed, and he looked into the rear view mirror to see who it was. The car was rushing towards his quite fast, and before he could react, the car dashed into his car giving him no chance to escape. The impact threw Arjun along with his friend Eshaan towards the dashboard. As they weren't wearing seat belts, they were thrown completely off balance. Arjun's luxurious car's safety air balloon did not inflate. Arjun's chest was pressed with the steering whereas Eshaan was lifted towards the windshield. Eshaan's head dashed into the glass, spurting his blood everywhere, and he became unconscious.

Arjun, due to the steering in his hand, was a little less injured as compared to Eshaan who lay there.

In anger, Arjun moved out of the car shouting, "Who the mother fucker is this? I was told that I will kill someone, and that is you now!" He came closer to the car behind his, which was badly damaged.

Arjun shivered for a second. The car which had dashed into his car was badly damaged. It would be a miracle for the driver to survive. As the smoke cleared, Arjun could see a girl in the car, badly injured. He concentrated hard on her face as blood was dripping from her face.

"Mahi!" he screamed.

"No one can ever defeat me!" Mahi looked at him and fell on the seat, unconscious.

Case no 242

Mathur's agile mind was already busy with the problem. Seeing his expression of concentration, Bhandey sat back and lit a cigarette with an unsteady hand. He had to wait several minutes before Mathur said, "I could find this murderer in a few days and put him behind bars. I have the men and organization to do it. That's why I am in the office. But this isn't the solution, I am afraid." He looked directly at Bhandey.

Bhandey handed him the file.

Sub Divisional Police Office Daryaganj.

Crime Review Note Of Police Station Main Metro Delhi Held By Undersigned On 30-06-2015.

A review of pending inquest proceedings was conducted by the undersigned on 30-06-2015. The following directions/ instructions were given in the meeting:

1. **Inquest vide DDR No.07 dated 11-05-2015, regarding the death of Singhal Family R/O Central Delhi, Daryaganj.**

I have gone through the CD file and found that there is insufficient material as well as statement of deceased further for registration of case. The photographs are placed in the CD file which indicates some suspicion. They have taken some poisonous substance which creates more doubts and needs to be verified from the watchman as well as from the other sources, before registration of case, matter requires to be investigated thoroughly on the following points:

a) What were the places of death, the body position at death?
b) Distance of workstation and residential complex and mode of drive?
c) Enquire from watchman whether the residence was locked/ open?
d) How many rooms were there in residential complex? Who was present in which room at the time of death? Enquire at what time who had left the room and behaviour of deceased on the day of death?
e) Telephone calls also securitized in detail.

The present I/O is directed to call neighbours and source person to verify the above-mentioned points and then go for registration of case.

NO: 242/SDR
Dated: 23/6/2015

Dy. Supdt. of Police,
SDPO Daryaganj.

Copy to:
1. Inspr. Gen. of Police JZ Daryaganj
2. Inspr. Gen. of Police C&R Daryaganj
3. Dy. Inspr.Genl.of Police ND Range Central Delhi
4. Sr. Supdt. of Police Daryaganj
5. Supdt. of Police Hqrs. Daryaganj
    .... for favour of kind information please.
6. SHO P/S Daryaganj for information and necessary action.

SDPO Daryaganj

Mathur opened his drawer and took out the photographs and the lens to re-check the photographs. His sharp eyes noticed an enormously high-ceilinged room that could house a hundred people. There was one photograph of the entrance to the crime scene. He gave a brief look at the stone wall surrounding the estate which was twenty feet high with cruel-looking steel barbs mounted along the top of the wall. He gave a brief look at the furniture – the wrought iron chairs and a tiny shield bearing the initials 'Best Sportsman – J---- School'. Since the photograph was not zoomed at the objects behind, the school's name was not clear. He opened his little diary from his pocket and noted down the little details he had observed.

Mahi and Arjun: Accidently an accident

The loud sound of the crash caught everyone's attention. The guard called the emergency. Joy got the news a minute later from other classmates ran towards the parking to handle the situation, but this time, his friends had crossed the limits and it was something which could not be taken care of. He found his friends at their worst. There was uneasiness on Arjun's face. As each second passed, their pain worsened and it worried Joy.

He waited for the ambulance to enter the school premises with the paramedic staff loaded with every kind of equipment. Looking at the situation and the blood loss, the staff suggested that everyone should be admitted to the hospital. Joy stood there confused; he joined in as a care taker and went along to the hospital.

The road seemed to be long and twisted. Joy kept looking at Arjun and Eshaan who remained motionless, and that made him nervous. The blood all over Mahi's clothes caused a cold lump of fear at the back of Joy's throat. He wedged his body close to her to give her support and held her hand tight.

Eshaan's wounds were deep and they would need stitches whereas Arjun only had some abrasions for which he was given first aid, but Mahi's situation was critical. Mahi was taken into the hospital's observation ward after first aid. Eshaan and Arjun were taken to the general ward.

The clock ticked and everything was quiet. Joy went back to the hostel to change his clothes. Arjun stood near Eshaan.

"Are you okay brother?" Eshaan asked.

"Yeah, just a little pain," he smiled shamelessly.

Arjun was afraid that Mahi would tell everyone that he had molested her and it would ruin his career.

"Did she say something?" Arjun asked.

"I don't know," Eshaan replied.

Then Arjun went out to the central porch of the hospital premises. In the adjacent room, Mahi was kept under observation. Sitting outside on the benches, he looked towards the staircase, thinking what could have been the consequences if the situation had gone from bad to worse. A kiss that was so expensive. At this moment, he was expecting a call from his parents. He was wondering why the hospital administration had not called their parents yet.

"I think this is the first time that I am feeling bad for someone," said Eshaan to Arjun as he came outside joining him.

"I too agree with you, but I must tell you, I think I am totally over this girl. She is too much."

"Still I think we should apologize once she comes into her senses." Arjun looked into Eshaan's eyes and this time he looked very serious.

"What is wrong in requesting for forgiveness if we are guilty? I think we should come forward." Arjun nodded in agreement to Eshaan's suggestion.

As expected, there was a call from his home.

"No mom, I am okay!" replied Arjun.

"I am not the one who crashed the car," he replied to his mom with anger. He knew his mother always scolded him for all those mistakes he made and for those that he did not.

"C'mon, for god's sake, leave me alone!" Arjun replied furiously as he knew he would never be able to convince his mother about his innocence.

"You are not going to get into the car again!" His mother was furious.

Arjun disconnected the line. The door facing him opened and an elderly man, wearing a black knitted sweater and a light grey over-coat came into the lobby. He moved with arrogance. In his right hand, he carried a bulky envelope. It was the principal who had just entered the hospital and silence prevailed. Arjun and Eshaan stood up; they knew this was going to be the end of Arjun's career. He knew if Mahi would say anything about the kiss, this would be a case of molestation. He crossed his fingers.

The long thin arrogant face, the lines around the weak, dry mouth, the smudges around the baggy eyes made the principal look unhappy.

"Are you okay, my son?" the principal looked at injuries and asked Eshaan who was in his good books.

"So, are you the culprit?" the principal looked at Arjun with rage.

"No, I am not," Arjun tried to skip the answer.

"Let's see what the girl has to say? This is the first time something bad has happened in the school and I am ashamed of it." Both Arjun and Eshaan kept quiet, because they were scared of what Mahi would say.

"If you are at fault, this is going to be your last year in the school," he instructed in a strict manner and went into the room where Mahi was kept under observation.

Arjun sat there outside the room, waiting for his punishment.

"Nothing can help me now," he confided to Eshaan.

"Let's hope for the best and prepare for the worst." He patted Arjun's back.

"We will always be friends." Arjun smiled. He knew there may be more doors opened for him if he would be thrown out of the school, but he wanted to stay with his V3 group.

"Take good care of yourself boys," the principal came out of the room, clutching his envelope and went away without saying anything much. It was now known to both of them that Mahi had saved them. Their smiles bounced off them like golf balls slamming against a wall.

"I am still confused. Why didn't she name us?" Arjun asked surprisingly.

"What can I say? I have been working over her details for the past two days for you and you idiotically tried to kiss her," Eshaan grilled him.

"Now don't try to be my mother," Arjun retaliated. "Give me the details!" he continued.

"Mahi is the daughter of a leading entrepreneur. She is a resident of Himachal Pradesh. Her mother died when she was only four years old. Her father remarried and Mahi didn't get along too well with the new mother. So she has been living against all odds, has learned to be independent. She excels in studies and is a state topper. Her father wanted her to join their business so she took admission here at our school at Shimla." Eshaan gave him the details.

"What about her personal life?" Arjun enquired.

"Well, she never had a boyfriend. Since she is a topper from her school, nobody either approached her or maybe some other reason, but I think we are nowhere close to her."

Arjun had been smiling sheepishly and Eshaan could not make head or tail out of it. "I think we should stop thinking about her or about taking any revenge," Eshaan said.

"Who is thinking about revenge? This is love!" Arjun put his hand over his head with a silly smile on his face.

"It is like two opposite people," Eshaan tried to make a point.

"I like her," Arjun replied.

"Well I can't say anything."

"You do one thing, let me know her dad's company's name. I will go check her assets and her company will deal with my father's company."

Arjun was wrong here, thinking about buying her with money. He did not know money could buy anything but love.

It had been a few days in the hospital, and Mahi was recovering steadily. One of her ribs had broken, so she was still in pain.

"Flowers ma'am!" The ward boy came with flowers. A lavish bunch of flowers met her gaze.

"Keep it there." She pointed towards the table.

"Who sent it?" Mahi was confused, as she was very new to the school and to the place and did not expect anyone to send her flowers.

"Your well-wishers perhaps."

"But who? Who gave it to you?" she asked again.

"Well there is a note in it I guess," he replied.

"Hand it here to me," Mahi took hold of the bouquet and searched for the sender.

"I think I like you." Mahi read and got the hint. It was none other than Arjun. She threw them over the side table and lay down in pain.

"Idiot," she whispered.

"Flowers, madam." Another person entered the room with flowers in his hand.

"Now who sent that?" Mahi babbled.

"I don't know madam, someone has sent these flowers too."

"You should not accept these flowers."

"Madam, but how can we say no to someone?"

"Ah! Okay, leave them on the table." The ward boy placed the flowers on the table.

"Don't you want to see who sent these?"

"No thanks!" she replied in anger. And the ward boy put the flowers over the table and left the room.

What the heck has happened to Arjun now? What is he up to? Mahi said to herself.

"Flowers, madam." A voice was heard, and as Mahi turned, someone was standing with flowers in his hand. It was Arjun.

"Arjun, now what is that for? Some cheap tactic by you, like in a Bollywood movie... you suck!" Mahi said as she was now tired of his efforts to reconcile.

"Well thanks Mahi for not telling the principal the truth." He was guilty and the guilt was visible on his face.

"It's okay Arjun. Look, we have no issues with each other, let's end it here. Let's just forget whatever happened," she ended the discussion.

A wave of silence prevailed in the room, forcing Arjun to leave without any more words.

Case no 242

Mathur sat in his office, staring out of the window, watching the traffic on the road. His face was stony, he was disappointed. He took a seal-skin cigar from his pocket, selected the cigar, nipped off the end with the cutter, then slowly and deliberately lit it. It was only when he was satisfied that the cigar was burning evenly that he looked at the case report left on his table, wiping his sweating face nervously with his handkerchief.

Sub Divisional Police Office Daryaganj.

Crime Review Meeting of Important Cases of Police Station Central Delhi, Main Metro Complex, Central Delhi and Daryaganj Held by undersigned On 14-06-2015.

Crime review meeting was held in the office of the undersigned regarding important cases including murder, rapes, theft, attempt to murder and other cases were discussed. The below mentioned SHOs of Sub Division attended the meeting along with CD files:

1. Inspr. Deepak Pathania SHO P/S Central Delhi
2. Inspr. Bharat Sharma SHO P/S Daryaganj
3. Inspr. Inderpal Singh SHO P/S Central Delhi
4. SI Ravi Singh SHO P/S Main Metro Complex

Bhandey entered and saw Mathur busy with the case report. He did not disturb him and quietly sat on the sofa, waiting to begin a conversation. He placed his briefcase on his knees and sat back, snubbed and silent. In his briefcase, he carried an envelope in which he had put the collected photographs of the other suspect, who was once Singhal's partner in the aviation industry. Bhandey had been asked to keep a watch on him and to take his photographs. Mathur knew Morgan because of his bad reputation. He had served five years in jail, and that he was violent and dangerous. He knew it would be a huge problem if Morgan was involved in the crime.

Bhandey handed over the envelope and Mathur opened it, taking a look at the photographs. The man in the photograph was tall with a fiddle-shaped face, widely spaced cold eyes, a jutting chin and a thin tight mouth.

"Do you think he can commit this crime?" Mathur asked. He was rocking himself back and forth, shaking his head.

"No, I don't think so. Murder is something too big for him," Bhandey replied.

"I have heard he has some moral courage. But still you never know whether he is bluffing." Bhandey added and shrugged his shoulders.

"What else do you have regarding this suspect?" Mathur pinned Morgan's photograph on his case board with the board-pin. A range of photographs – in color, sepia, black and white – adorned the wall. Now, both the men were silent and preoccupied with their thoughts.

"We still do not have Morgan's call records," Mathur said with a waspish note in his voice.

"I am still working on it," Bhandey spoke slowly and distinctly, with a threat in every word and wandered to the door.

As he was about to leave; Mathur suggested, "I would suggest you keep a copy of these photographs with you and we will destroy the photographs and films later, before submitting this case to the court. Such a case report will be more puzzling at the time of hearing." He turned and looked enquiringly at him. There was a steely gleam in his eyes that told Bhandey he was dead serious about this case.

"If he is going to be our suspect, then we will delete other suspects from the list and he can further give the lucid report regarding Morgan if needed," he added and Bhandey left the office.

Mathur quickly read the other case and finally drafted his case file.

Case FIR No.242/2015 u/s 174/RPC.

This case was registered on 27-04-2015 and is being investigated by SHO P/S Central Delhi. Perusal of CD file and observed that the case is pending only for want of medical report. SHO has been directed to depute a responsible officer for obtaining the pending medical report. SHO is further directed to ascertain the call details of all the relatives of deceased person and friends of deceased person. The case is very important in nature. SHO is advised to constitute a team and put them on the job and get the feedback every alternate day and also appraise the progress of the case weekly to the undersigned. SHO is directed to approach the concerned authorities, get the medical report and close the case on merits at the earliest.

Dy.Supdt.of Police,
SDPO Daryaganj.

No.:- /SDR
Dtd:-

Copy to:
1. Inspr. Gen. of Police, JZ Central Delhi
2. Dy. Inspr. Gen. of Police, JK Range Central Delhi
3. Sr. Supdt. of Police, Central Delhi
4. Supdt. of Police, Hqr. Central Delhi
    ....for favour of kind inf. please.
5. SHO P/S Daryaganj/Main Metro Police Station/Central Delhi /Central Delhi for further necessary action.

SDPO Daryaganj

The case reports were on the table. Mathur knew that the police still didn't think it was a suicide case and there was a lot of pressure due to the interference of the media. He also knew that the police did not want to look at the case taking the help of a special CID officer and wanted to solve it on their own. It was clear that a usual drug was not used. If it was, it had to be sleeping pills, which were easily available, and then it would be a pure case of suicide.

"Why would they kill themselves with such a drug?" Mathur asked himself.

"May I enter, Mathur?" asked the CID officer. He was a short bird-like man, wearing rimless glasses. He looked more like a successful banker rather than the shrewd, ruthless senior officer of an extremely efficient organization whose secret mechanizations and surreptitious activities were so vast that only a few people could know how powerful it was! He looked directly at Mathur, "You and I are friends. We have things in common. You may have done a lot for this case, and I would more than welcome the opportunity to do something for you. But you have enemies. Some of your men do not want you to work on this case. They don't agree to your view… that's their privilege. It would be impossible for you to use your network on this case or may be some of your agents are deliberately leaking news to the media." He rubbed his hands over his face, and then lifted his shoulders, giving a resigning shrug.

But Mathur knew he was playing a mind game with him; they were not on the same side. They were competing with each other. He had orders not to be in touch or take help from the CID officers for this case. They knew each other's capabilities and also knew that to solve this case alone and not together was a challenge, but they had no other option.

"Yes!" He offered him a seat. Mathur did not like his presence, but due to decorum, he had to remain calm and silent for any clue.

"So did the report come?" the CID officer asked him to show what was in his hand and also looked around his office and at the other files on the table.

"No," Mathur lied as he wanted him to solve this case the other way without any manipulations as told by his seniors. Both looked at each other and silence prevailed as if the CID officer already knew about the reports.

"So, Officer, what do you think the case might be? I mean suicide is a very lame excuse," the CID officer asked.

"Please, I think you are influenced by the media. This is actually a murder," Mathur said as he now wanted to change the topic. He knew very well that the CID officer wanted to attain information and nothing else.

"But still, do you think it is business rivalry?" He raised his eyebrows in disbelief. "I mean, if you see the company was running on deficit, this is something which hints that the major investor might have…" The CID officer was clever enough to confuse Mathur.

"But do you really think a person who is a sleeping partner of a silent investor will take such huge a risk for money and do something like this?" Mathur counter questioned. "A clever murder," he added as an afterthought.

"Did you say murder!" The CID officer made an eye contact to find out whether he was trying to confuse him or was he really giving him a hint.

"Can I please go to the washroom? Excuse me!" Breaking the eye contact, Mathur tried to skip what he had said a minute ago and left his table, putting the reports inside his drawer. While doing so, Mathur unlocked the bottom drawer of his desk and switched on a video recorder which had a sensitive microphone and camera. His gadget was so sensitive that it didn't need leads. The button camera was already placed with an angle to record his cabin.

He left the cabin, and as soon as the CID officer heard the water running, he jumped to the other side. From his overcoat, he took out the pen camera and clicked a few photographs of the report saving the time to read it and left the office.

The magic eye of the button camera recorded everything. By the time Mathur reached his table, he saw the drawer had been opened, the files had been hastily drawn out and the CID officer was nowhere in sight. He knew that the CID officer had flipped through his files. He opened the drawer and restored them back. It looked like somebody had hurriedly kept those files back. They were also not in order, which Mathur was very particular about.

He turned off the video recorder, and turned on his TV unit, switched to the recorder channel, and clicked on the destination file, and played it in slow-motion. He was satisfied that he had an excellent recording of the CID officer tampering with his office files. He then copied the particular scene on a memory card for the records, took a large envelope, sealed the memory card in it with a tape and wrote: 'CID hunt at the office 1:30 p.m'. He put the envelope into his pocket. This was a cunning move.

"Bastard!" he said to the CID officer who had left the building with the photos of the report in his camera. Mathur settled down on his table and took the files out to look for any clue the CID officer might discover before him. He didn't want to lose.

Virat and Payal

Virat was possessive about this photograph and quite restless to know more about the girl. He had no clue; most of the staff members in the school were not seniors and kept changing every semester. It was pure destiny that he had come across a person who had some issue with the school about which no one was ready to talk. He was determined to seek answers. Only one person from whom he could ferret out the information was the librarian, who was one of the oldest staff members in the school. He finally broached the topic in front of him.

"Sir, can you help me?" Virat pleaded to the librarian, his only hope.

"What is it?" asked the librarian in an obliging manner. He was very strict and did not interact much with the students. It needed a lot of courage to approach him to ask about a girl, but Virat took the chance.

"I need a little information, sir," said Virat trying to convince him.

"Like what? Is it about a book or some syllabus?" The librarian stopped and looked up from the same angle, wearing his miniature sized glasses.

"I need to know about a girl," said Virat. He knew he sounded silly asking a librarian about it, but he was desperate to know anything about her. He had to take the risk.

The librarian looked at him suspiciously. "What do you mean?"

"No, I mean I want a little detail about this photograph." Virat placed the picture in front of the librarian. He cringed at his question and he could easily see a desperate look of need in Virat's eyes. The librarian gave an unexpected expression; he snatched the photograph from him, threw it into his drawer and kept himself busy with the work.

"Out!" He gave no importance to him, and kept himself busy with the work he was previously busy with. He did not look at him due to the fear of giving away any information.

"Sir?" Virat folded his hands to plea.

"I said out!" He did not even care to look up and kept doing his work as if he was hiding something. He seemed angry, very angry. Virat stayed there for a while, helpless, but then he left the office.

Virat was fuming, but he knew he could not do anything. He thought for a while of a way to get the picture back, but he knew it was impossible to steal it; he knew such things happen only in movies. Virat was angry as he entered his hostel room. He wanted the picture back; she was the only one he had to talk to. It was a part of his daily routine now. He lay on the bed, but remained restless. He could not think of a way out to get it back. He then stood up and looked himself in the mirror. In a sudden fit of rage, he threw the dustbin on the mirror, breaking it into many pieces. He, in resentment, threw everything he could get hold of against the wall.

Finally, his heart shattered into pieces, his morale with it. He sat in the corner of the room and cried out loud. He was alone once again. The aura created by the photograph in his room was gone. It was like the loss of a friend.

Mahi and Arjun

Everyone was at the canteen. Arjun entered looking for Mahi. He pulled out a chair and sat opposite her at the nearby table. He stared admiringly at her, watching the way her pink lips moved, and her breasts lifted as she raised her arms. He leaned forward and gave a slip to the girl sitting next to him to pass it on to Mahi. "Can you pass it over to the girl sitting next to you?"

"What?" The girl exclaimed looking at him.

Eshaan was sitting with him and was confused. "I tell you, I like this girl." Arjun explained with a smile on his face.

"Pass it, Madam," he again requested.

Everyone was surprised to see Arjun so courteous. He looked different, as if after the accident, he had begun to realize the value of things. As the slip reached in the hands of Mahi, she looked at Arjun who was sitting diagonally. She smiled at him and tore the slip. Arjun sat back with a grin. Mahi did not respond, instead gave him a cold shoulder.

"What did you write in the slip, Arjun?" Eshaan asked.

"Nothing much. I just requested her for a date." Arjun stared at Mahi while Eshaan was confused about what was happening to Arjun these days.

"Do you think after so much that has happened, she will trust you?" Eshaan exclaimed.

"Well, I have turned over a new leaf…now she has to trust me," Arjun suggested.

Arjun did not want things to go like this. He tried to speak to Mahi once their class ended.

"Hey, Mahi!" Arjun called out her name. Mahi slowed down and Arjun came running to catch up with her.

"Hi," Arjun said huffing and puffing.

"Hello." Mahi kept walking, though a little slower.

"Where are you going?" he asked.

"Do you know there is a library in the school?" Mahi asked.

"Yeah," he replied.

"Well I am going there." She quickened her steps. "At least you know where it is," she taunted.

"Can I join you?" Arjun again requested.

"Have you paid the school fees?" Mahi asked.

"Yeah!"

"Then why you are taking my permission to visit the library; it's all yours!"

"I know more chilled out places here in school," said Arjun.

"Look Arjun, I have wasted one whole month in the hospital, so for god's sake, leave me and let me study. You have no issues with the studies and will join your dad's business," she said it all in a single breath.

"Well, I have an offer for you and for your dad's company too!" Arjun said without thinking.

"So you think I have not taken your name to the principal because of this?" Mahi said angrily. "Arjun, I just gave you one last chance so that you can change yourself; be loyal to your father and enjoy this trip your father has invested upon," and the conversation ended as Mahi reached the library.

"You know Mahi, I like you." Arjun smiled to cover the embarrassment. Mahi waited outside the library to pen down the entry and Arjun, who was new to the library, entered the library without penning down the entry.

"Sir, kindly enter your name," the guard stopped him.

"What? Is this necessary?" He was confused. "Is this a bank or what?" he shouted.

"Shut up! It is a bank of knowledge," Mahi replied irritatingly.

Mahi came from behind, "Arjun, just follow the protocol and don't shout; it is a library and we have to keep quiet here."

"Okay okay!" he whispered and they both entered the library.

"Here, to this section," Mahi showed him the way. She knew if she did not help the poor chap, he would get into another argument with someone.

"Yeah," he replied.

Mahi searched for a book she had wanted to read and took a seat. Arjun too did the same. Uninterested, he tried to pass time which ticked very slowly. Arjun took out his mobile and read a message.

Where are you? Eshaan wanted to know.

I am in the library, he texted back. Arjun turned on a game on his mobile. As the game started, and more so unknowingly, since his mobile was not on silent mode, the game music started to play loudly. Before Arjun could react and take hold of the situation, the librarian came with a sniffing attitude.

"Out!" he ordered in anger.

"Sir…" Arjun switched off his mobile in embarrassment.

"Out, I said, else I will throw you out myself!" Arjun had no choice but to leave the place, though he wanted to be with Mahi.

Gosh! Why did I do that? he scolded himself.

Suddenly, he got an idea. He took a copy from a student passing by and tore a page on which he wrote:

Please, I am getting bored here. Meet me in the coffee shop near the garden.

He stood near the window where Mahi was busy reading. Mahi did not notice Arjun standing there. Arjun gently knocked on the windowpane and Mahi looked at him. She read the note he was holding up, nodded a 'yes' and requested him to put the paper down lest someone else saw it. Arjun signalled to her that he was going to the coffee shop. But Mahi was so engrossed in her book that only after an hour did she remember that Arjun would be waiting for her. It was raining outside and was cold out there. The coffee shop was an open shop, so she closed her book and ran towards the garden to look for him. Mahi did not expect Arjun to be sitting there after an hour and that too in the rain, but Arjun was still there, drenched.

"What the hell! Couldn't you go back to your hostel?" she said huffing as she reached him. Arjun was shivering in the cold.

"Coffee?" Arjun asked.

"Are you insane Arjun? This is not love; this is purely infatuation," Mahi tried to explain.

"If it is not love, then I will never fall in love again!" Arjun looked serious.

"Look Arjun, we are different," Mahi had tears in her eyes.

"What different?" he asked. "We both are human beings! I know you like me too Mahi, and that is the reason you are here," Arjun said.

"Is it the rich and the poor thing?" he tried to probe because she hadn't said a word.

"No, I don't like you; this is the reason," Mahi replied back.

"But why?"

"Because you are not my kind of a man... you drink, you dope..." She gave him the exact reason.

"Really?" Arjun for the first time repented his deeds.

Arjun was disappointed; an act which he thought made him look very cool was actually turning out to be something no girl would like. Every girl likes a boyfriend who has qualities similar to her father. Arjun had nothing to say to her after listening to this, so he left the place.

Days passed, but Mahi did not see Arjun again anywhere, not even for classes.

Case no 242

Mathur took out a cigarette from his pocket, slowly and deliberately lit it. He released the smoke down his nostrils, eyeing the burning end of his cigarette.

People like to be big fish in a small pond, he thought and then took the new reports from the table in his hand:

Police Station, Central Delhi.

Case FIR No.242/2015 u/174/RPC.

This case was registered on 14-04-2015 and is being investigated by ASI Bishan Dass. Perusals of CD file and observed that the case is pending to detail and identify the accused person. SHO has been directed to make sincere efforts to make identification and arrest the absconding accused and produce the challan of the case in the court of law within ten days and furnish compliance report.

NO: 242/SDR
Dated: 23/6/2015

Dy. Supdt. of Police,
SDPO Daryaganj

Copy to:
1. Inspr. Gen. of Police JZ Daryaganj
2. Inspr. Gen. of Police C&R Daryaganj
3. Dy. Inspr. Gen.of Police ND Range Central Delhi
4. Sr. Supdt. of Police Daryaganj
5. Supdt. of Police Hqrs. Daryaganj
   .... for favour of kind information please.
6. SHO P/S Daryaganj for information and necessary action
   SDPO Daryaganj

There had been no progress in the case, and to make things more interesting, news channels had now started covering the scams the royal family had been involved in, complicating the case further. There was a political bent too and now it was time that Mathur went for the kill, but reporters were continuously following him at every step.

No one was permitted to enter the crime scene as it had been sealed by the Intelligence Bureau. For the sake of the investigation, Mathur knew he had to break the law himself to solve this case. He knew that there were a few more clues which were hidden inside the building.

He had to make a smart move. He was so unnerved, he could no longer sit at the table. He closed the door and went to fetch his suitcase which was kept behind his office couch. He tossed out its contents on the table. He pressed the tiny spring hidden under the lining of the case and bottom of the case clicked open, revealing a tray in which were kept his professional weapons. They consisted of a Walther automatic pistol with a magazine capacity of eight rounds, a razor sharp doubled-bladed stabbing knife and a tear gas bomb. He always travelled well equipped. He took the pistol, loaded it, hid it under his tuxedo, moved out of his office and walked across the narrow street, where he had parked his car. He got in and waited. In ten minutes, he saw a reporter who was searching for him, sauntering down the street. He was wearing a short leather coat over his t-shirt and jeans. He was smoking, with one hand thrust into his coat pocket.

Mathur started his car. He saw the same guy cross the road and get into a van. He turned left, allowing two cars to be between his car and the reporter's van. He turned right and drove a few metres down the busy road. With the skill that was his natural talent, he skipped the cars across the main street, and into another side street, slackening the speed slightly, flicking on his headlights and flicking them off immediately as he drove across the intersections. He stared at the rearview mirror to see if he was being followed.

Forced to continue down the street through the traffic, the reporter looked around; he had lost sight of him. Mathur also noticed that the van was out of sight, so he could now go to the crime scene. It took an hour for him to reach the spot. It was late at night and everything moved slowly in the capital.

Mathur decided to find his way by foot instead of taking his police jeep. He made his first stop at a shop nearby to buy a cigarette. The shopkeeper had hooded eyes, a thick hooked nose and deeply tanned complexion of a man who had travelled a lot in the sun.

"A pack of Four Square," he asked for a pack of his brand of cigarettes.

"Here sir," said the cigarette seller, who was also one of his spies.

"So any news about the case?"

"Nothing Babuji, apart from the regular conversations about the case," he answered.

Mathur gave a hundred rupee note to the seller and left the spot.

Mathur had a different way of thinking. His modus operandi was also very different and far better than any agency in the country. The last case he had solved was about a drug dealer who happened to have political connections which led to his posting in a far flung area. His truthfulness had always got him into trouble. Now, this was the most important case for him which was going to take him back to regular office.

He crossed the road and made way to a dark spot. He stood there for a while to observe the security, then flicked his half-smoked cigarette on the street.

Since the building was sealed, there were a few officers and a PSO who stood on duty. He stayed out in the darkness watching the activity outside. He was glad to see there were no search dogs. However, there were plenty of men and he made a rough count – possibly fifteen or sixteen. It was difficult to count them as they kept disappearing and reappearing in the light. Finally he made a decision to step in. He skipped the sight and broke the glass window with a push. His heart thumped sluggishly for a fraction of a second and his hands went moist. It was dark and damp and very quiet, so he slowly made an entry into the building unnoticed.

To the left at the entrance was a big study room. It had undergone certain changes; there lay the canvas deck-chair that had once served as an armchair. Adjacent to the wall was spotted a deep reclining padded-chair and a big settee. He took out a little torch from his pocket and cleared his way towards the murder spot and started with his investigation from the main hall. There was a splendid Bukhara rug on the floor; its rich hues did a lot to give a tone of luxury to this otherwise dark-looking room. Looking for some clues, he opened the TV unit drawers, looked for blood stains over the rug and searched for any evidence left behind.

Then he went to the bedroom to look for evidence in the drawers of the study table and searched for adjustments made to the bed sheet. He went to the dressing table, looked for empty cigarette butts thrown into the trash basket. He went to see if there were any blood stains in the sink. These were vital as these would indicate if any forceful activity had taken place. But he found nothing, absolutely nothing! He went back to the porch. As Inspector Mathur reached the main hall of the building again, he heard some suspicious movement in the building. This made him very anxious. *Why would someone enter a sealed building at this hour and by which route?*

He quickly turned off his torch and stayed there quietly. He believed in the theory that no crime is done with perfection. So, if it was a murder, the murderer could enter the building again to look for any mistakes he might have committed.

Thinking that the murderer could be violent, he searched for his 9mm loaded pistol in his tuxedo. This was his personal one and not a regular duty revolver. He then hid himself behind a wall and leant forward to take a view. He confirmed the presence of someone by the sound of footsteps heading towards the kitchen; he took a stance for his next step. He could feel his eyes trying to penetrate the heavy veil of darkness. His armpits became damp. Surely he could feel the fear! Mathur was sure now, so he unlocked his gun and aimed to fire. He was expecting a few return shots if he fired first. And he knew well that if something like that happened at this critical stage, the case would be messed up even more. Reaching the kitchen, he leaned to the other side of the wall to have a better view, while he could see a shadow searching for something in the bin. He aimed at the culprit and started to head towards him. With the sweat running down his face, Mathur kept looking at him. All he knew was there was someone standing in the kitchen who shouldn't be there. He was unprepared. Mathur knew he should not move very quickly, but the panicky movement alerted the stranger. Mathur slowed down and went behind a chair with a cautious tip-toe and sat there to check. The door closed softly somewhere to his right. He saw a shadow flit across the wall. The shadow stopped for a moment; perhaps the intruder was deciding what to do next. Then the shadow lengthened as the man moved away from the wall. He was heading towards the other side.

"Hands up!" Mathur ordered him as he did not want to start firing. He himself came out from the little space behind the chair where he was hiding. Mathur had an ominous feeling that he had landed himself straight into trouble again.

The indistinct shadow of the man now froze with his hands raised. Mathur searched for his torch, and lit it up.

"Turn around and show me your face, otherwise I will shoot you," he shouted, aiming his gun over him with his voice raised to show his confidence.

The moment stood still; the clock ticked slowly. This was the moment when either this case would be solved in one single run or he would mess up.

"Turn around, I say," he said in anger. His heart hammered and his mouth was dry.

The man turned around. "What the hell are you doing here?" Mathur looked at him holding his gun down. He was none other than the CID officer who had come to his office!

He was the last man on earth Mathur expected or wanted to see. He knew immediately that the CID officer had gone too far this time.

"Look, we are on the same side," the CID officer tried to convince him.

"This is against the law. You don't have the permission to enter this sealed building, and it is under my department," he said and asked him to walk to the centre of the room.

"But you don't have permission as well," he retorted. "Do you still want to take me into your custody?" the CID officer asked. Mathur knew it would be a shame for his department if this came to light, so he decided to play a mind game with him. He knew it was easy for him to manipulate him at that moment. Before the CID officer could react, suddenly a noise came from the other side of the building and they both ran towards it together. There was somebody else present in the building and it was that clue which they both did not want to miss.

Mathur ran from the other side while the CID officer ran out of the building to get hold of the culprit. Mathur knew that if at this stage the criminal was caught, credit will be given to his department; and if in any case there was another goof up, he would be not be given any further chance to investigate this case in the building. So it was his only attempt.

The CID officer could not find anything; it was just a dry branch from the tree which had brushed the windowpane due to the strong breeze. Mathur quickly went to the kitchen to look at what the CID officer was searching for in the bin.

"Apples?" he asked himself, "Loads of them!"

He quickly took one out with his gloves not to destroy the fingerprints and dropped it into a plastic packet, keeping in mind that no damage should be done to the evidence for the pathological test.

While Mathur was collecting the samples, six heavily-built men wearing masks entered the house.

"Caught you! You can't run!" One of the security officers who came into the building with the torch shouted to check if someone was inside the building.

Mathur rushed across the kitchen, jerked open the door and dashed into the large garden. And he wasted no time to leave the building with what he had found, carefully keeping himself out of sight of the duty officers.

The next day, Mathur sent the apple and the other samples to the lab for further testing and he sat with Bhandey for the next case report.

Sub Divisional Police Office Daryaganj.

Crime Review Meeting of Police Station Main Metro Central Delhi, Daryaganj and Central Delhi held by the undersigned on 06-06-2015.

Crime review meeting of heinous offences/ public importance cases has already been held and necessary directions were given to SHOs vide this office No 1532-35/SDR dated 20-05-2015. Today the crime meeting of major murder cases, accident cases, land dispute and minor offence cases and followed by a work shop on professional techniques of investigation of accident cases was organized. The below mentioned I.Os of different police stations of sub division Daryaganj attended the crime meeting/ workshop.

Whereas for the case no 242, further evidences have been collected from the bin which include:
1. Cotton swabs - 2 in nos.
2. Vegetable peels
3. Apples left outs - 6 in nos.

All the evidences have been submitted to the pathologist for tests.

Further the I/O diploids for the investigation in various stations are:
1. ASI Tarem Lal P/S Main Metro Station
2. ASI Som Nath P/S Main Metro Station
3. ASI Gopal Singh P/S Main Metro Station
4. ASI ChoorMani P/S Central Delhi
5. IHC Ajay Bharti P/S Central Delhi
6. HC Tarsem Lal P/S Central Delhi
7. ASI Tilak Raj P/S Daryaganj
8. ASI Subash Chander P/S Daryaganj
9. HC Bhola Nath P/S Daryaganj
10. ASI Sat Paul P/S Central Delhi

Police Station Daryaganj
1. **Case FIR No.242/2015 u/s 279/337/RPC**.
In this case, medical report has been obtained. The complaint party has not pursued the case, no witnesses has been examined. I.O stated that the complainant has not produced any witnesses, but in my opinion. I.O should verify the facts from spot about the incident. It is not necessary to produce the witnesses by the complainant. Only examination of witnesses is pending. I.O is directed to verify the facts of the case and conclude the investigation. Perusal of CD files of above mentioned cases and observed that most of the cases are pending for want of medical as well as postmortem reports. However, I.O of the cases have been directed to approach the concerned authorities, get the

medical and postmortem reports and finalize the cases on merits within ten days and report compliance.

Perusal of CD file and above mentioned cases and observed that the investigation of case figuring No. 14 closed as challan for arrest of one accused is pending in each case cited at figuring No.15 and 16. However, I.Os have been directed to put in sincere efforts to make their best and produce the needful investigation of these cases in the court of law within ten days.

Dy. Supdt. of Police
SDPO Daryaganj.

No.: /SDR

Dtd:

Copy to:
1. Sr. Supdt. of Police, Central Delhi
2. Supdt. of Police, Hqr. Central Delhi
    …….. for favour of kind inf. please.
3. SHO P/S Main metro Station/Central Delhi /Daryaganj/ Central Delhi for further necessary action.

SDPO Daryaganj

Virat and Payal

After the incident and the loss of the picture, Virat appeared to be an odd blend of restlessness, dullness, depression, and apart from that, it seemed that there surfaced a sentimental streak in him. The bad dreams had gone, but the girl in the photograph occupied his mind. He slept as if he had an uneasy drug dose and its traces could be easily noted by the puffiness under his eyes.

"Virat, are you taking drugs? Answer me Virat?" asked Payal as she had not been able to trace him for the last two days.

Virat was depressed. What the librarian had done was heart breaking for a teenager. He desperately wanted the picture back but he was helpless, he could not do anything else than repent. He asked Karan too about it, but he pleaded with Virat to not do something idiotic which would spoil his father's image as he was already in the midst of trouble.

"You need a psychologist," Payal bowled at him again with her flat statement which always irritated Virat.

It was hard for Virat to end this relationship. He knew it would be hard for Payal to accept the rejection. And he would also feel bad; memories of their togetherness were in their minds since years and her loving gestures couldn't be forgotten so easily. But her school-mistress attitude was unbearable, so he finally decided to break up.

"We are breaking up Payal," said Virat very confidently.

"Why, what?" She was confused, but Virat was more confident this time.

Both of them stood still. Virat looked into Payal's eyes; she had tears in them. The pain of being rejected. Virat was finally courageous and hurt enough to confess that he needed time and space.

"Do you love someone else?" Payal asked.

Virat stepped back and turned to leave. But Payal ran towards him and stopped him from leaving without an answer.

"I want an answer Virat," Payal shouted in anger.

"I do." Finally the storm broke and Payal had her worst nightmare confirmed.

"Who is that bitch?" she yelled.

Virat slapped her. "Don't you dare call her a bitch; I am telling you to stay away from her. I love her and I don't need to disclose her identity to you," he screamed.

"But who the hell is she?" Payal was not a girl to turn away easily. She too responded with anger. She knew Virat was dealing with some kind of a psychological problem.

"The girl in the photograph, I will show you…" He reminded her about the photograph.

"That hallucination!"

"She is real and I am going to find her." Virat said and moved away.

"Come on, Virat! You need a psychologist, and everything will be okay." Payal came close to hug him.

"Nothing will be okay, I think everything between us is over. I don't feel anything anymore," Virat moved away from Payal.

"C'mon, I am your girlfriend and you are leaving me for a hallucination. I will help you come out of it," she continued. "Trust me." She held his hand close to her heart.

"No, let me go,"Virat took his hand away. Payal was astounded.

"Bastard, you will come back to me and I will show you who I am!" She screamed with confidence but Virat went to the library. Payal could not believe that Virat was in love with a girl he did not know or had ever talked to and was leaving his girlfriend who had stood by him through all the good and bad times. Virtual versus reality.

Few days passed, but nothing changed between Virat and Payal. But his desire to search for the girl in the photograph increased. Virat started spending most of the time in the library whereas Payal kept on crying for him. Payal knew that Virat had some serious disorder and a troubled family background, but as days passed, this feeling of love turned into hatred. Payal was finally gone from his life.

Sunk deep into sadness, one day with a heavy heart, Virat went to the library looking for that novel in which he had found the photograph of the girl. He took the novel and started looking at the back about the information with an attempt to find out who had referred this book, but he could not find anything more than the school codes. These codes were difficult to crack. All Virat needed to do was to be at the same wavelength to find this girl whom he had started to love. He knew he was just a step away from solving this puzzle.

Looking at the codes closely in an attempt to decode them, suddenly a book fell from the shelf, and to his surprise, it turned out to be another link to the investigation. It was the yearly school magazine which he had completely forgotten about. The school had been publishing such books for the past few years where group photographs of students were published. He began to flip the pages faster. *I should have thought about this a long time back.* Virat smiled to himself.

He turned over to the last pages to check for the school group photographs. Only photographs of 10th to 12th were included here. He looked for various sections and finally he got what he was searching for. It was the perfect clue. He tore the picture. Now he just needed to find the name and the address of the girl from the register. He noted down the year.

At the back of the book he noted down the name of the person who had issued the book. He thoroughly went for the year when it was issued. Since it was not a subject book, it was not issued often.

"Roll no 5-year 2005: Roll no 22-year 2006…" he went reading the whole list of students who had issued the book that year; finally, he got what he was searching for: Roll no 39-year2007."

Well it was the time when this girl must have studied in the school according to the school group photograph. The school rules were very strict for novels which were not related to the school curriculum; only the 11 and 12th standard students could read this kind of stuff. So it was now evident that this girl he was looking for was Roll no 39 in the year 2007.

He had never felt so happy; it was like an achievement. After this clue, now he only had to go through the school records to find out the name of this girl. And with the help of the name, year and roll number, it would be easy to find the address or any other contact information.

He calculated her age; this girl was eight years older than him according to the records. The love story was getting more confusing. There were fewer chances that this girl would be unmarried. Virat was still very curious to know more about the girl and the inquisitiveness to meet her was now somewhat bridged.

Case no 242

Before the CID officer or Mathur could reach any closer to solving the case and could get any more clues, the dawn in the capital broke with the news of the murder of another businessman.

The news flashed all over the TV screens for the second biggest unsolved second degree murder case in the country. The last case was nowhere close to being solved. This was becoming a shame for the various departments whereas pressure started building up from the political parties.

It was also not clear if both the murders had something in common. But since they had taken place in the capital, the media attention was inevitable. It was now in the news that there was a serial killer in Delhi and that the administration was not being able to do anything to catch him. The front page of major newspapers concentrated on the murder. There were pictures of the crime scene and the blood stains. Every newspaper had their own story and assumptions defining different angles and predictions. The police headquarters were offering lakhs of rewards for any information that would give them a lead to the case.

Meanwhile at the police station, Bhandey came running with the newspaper in his hand. Mathur read the news and asked, "How did they get these pictures of the crime scene?"

He threw the newspaper aside, went to the cupboard and took out his briefcase. Bhandey had stripped off the two buttons of his shirt; his hairy chest was perspiring.

"Some kind of security failure," he replied and the office phone rang.

"Hello," Mathur greeted.

"Mathur, this is a shame for the department. There is another brutal murder in this area, what has happened to officers like you?" It was the first call of the morning from the superior, so Bhandey quietly left the office.

Mathur did not have an explanation, not yet. "Inspector, for case no 242, I have to address people every day; everything is so complicated and now one more murder... how will I handle the situation? We also have political pressure which has polluted the case. I want results!" said the senior inspector as Mathur put down the phone. He hopelessly stared at the dial. He made up his mind to get ready for action; he was now being given charge of the second murder in the city, further complicating case no 242. It was a huge responsibility and he would not goof it up, no matter what happened.

Assumptions that both the cases were related were doing the rounds as both victims were millionaires and their kids were school friends, alleged for the rape of a minor.

He sat on his chair and took out a cigarette. He studied the flame before leaning forward to dip the end of the cigarette into the ash tray. He now lit the lighter and looked at the flame. He saw the flame to be far from steady and realized that his hands were shaking. He snuffed out the flame and sat back, forcing a grin. He knew if he would go by this angle to the case, then he would make the case more complicated. He disapproved of such statements, but still had to visit the girl's house once.

He went to the society where the girl lived. The road to the house was narrow and at the end of the road, an old car was parked. He then took a sensitive button microphone which was cordless and switched it on. He tapped the microphone gently to make sure the recorder reacted, then clipped the microphone over his wrist watch and covered the watch with his frayed shirt sleeve. He was now ready to knock on the door.

Mathur went to the building where this girl who had been raped a few years back lived or used to live. There was a slotted window which gave him a direct view inside the house.

"Yes?" Someone came out asking.

"I am Inspector Mathur," he introduced himself. And while he gave his introduction, he tried to steal a look inside the house. It was a small unfurnished room with a short spiral staircase, leading to another floor of the house.

"Look at this photograph, have you seen this girl?" he asked.

"We are new here. We have taken this apartment just a few days back." Mathur got a dry reply.

"And did you see this girl when you talked to the landlord?" he inquired.

"No sir, this apartment belongs to an old man. I can provide you with his number."

The tenants gave him the phone number which Mathur noted down in his little investigation diary.

Before he could leave the place, the media was waiting for him, wanting answers. He knew this case was now getting more complicated.

"Sir, did you find any new clue in this case?" asked one of the senior reporters from a very reputed news channel.

"Why did you visit this place? Do you think the girl who was raped lived here was actually…?" asked one more reporter.

"Look, the court had acquitted those guys and it was not a case of rape. The case you are referring to was a drug and force case where these innocent millionaires were blackmailed for money. When they did not hand over the money, the girl said she had been raped. This case is an old case and had ended. Case no 242 is a different one and we are looking at it with a different angle."

There was quite a bit of chaos and a whole lot of questions. "It may be related to a business rivalry," he added. Mathur was smart enough to confuse the media.

"You mean to say that the business in which the accused rapist and one who was raped eight years back were involved?" questions showered from every end.

"I told you just now, it was not a rape case. The court had acquitted them," Mathur said and stepped out.

"But sir, what about the new murder that happened last night?" asked one of the media reporters from the back to which Mathur had no answer.

Leaving their questions unanswered, he went to his car and drove away from the scene. As he drove to the left after crossing the narrow street, a Volkswagen car stood by the roadside near the imposing entrance of an old building.

A silver-haired small man, wearing a shabby suit was working on the engine. Another nondescript-looking man sat in the driver's seat, smoking. This was the CID officer who had loosened a sparking-plug of the car which gave an appearance of a breakdown. Mathur gave a glance to the scene which looked a little forged; he rubbed his jaw as he thought. He sped up his car and left for the police station. He knew there was someone else too who was following him other than the media. He was a trained agent. The CID officer slammed down the cover over the engine and went to the building.

At the police station

"Sir, reports." One of the junior officers handed Mathur the samples of the apple given to the pathologist.

He called up Daisy, "Hello, what does positive mean here?"

"It means the apples have a drug coating. The family members in the case 242 must have eaten them and were killed," she replied.

Mathur was buzzed at how clever the murderer was to inject the drug in an apple.

"How could this be done?"

"By someone who knew they were going to eat those apples."

The modus operandi of the murderer was known but the murderer was roaming free in the streets.

"Where can you get this drug?" Mathur asked.

"From the laboratory, but you need a prescription," she added and the conversation ended.

"Get me details of the laboratories in the town," he told the other officer working under him.

In a few days, the details were on his table. Surprisingly the drug had not been sold since the past few months. The plan was an old one. And to find the apple seller was another option, but Mathur knew this was also an idiotic option to follow. Case no 242 was getting more complicated, whereas the corresponding case was becoming one of the hot topics of the town.

Mathur started with the second reporting of the murder.

Sub Divisional Police Office, Daryaganj

Sr-A Police Station Daryaganj. District Central Delhi.

Subject: - **Inquest proceedings U/S 174/Crpc into the death of Satyankar Gowerker S/o Aatil Gowerker R/O Daryaganj Tehsil Central Delhi.**
District Central Delhi, initiated vide DDR No. 06 dated 07-09-2015, P/S Daryaganj.

1. Name of the person who   : Police Station Daryaganj.
   lodged the report
2. Date of occurrence.   : 07-09-2015.
3. Date of report and time   : 07-09-2015.
4. Name of the deceased with   : Rishi Gowerker S/O
   full particulars   Satyankar Gowerker S/O
                                     Aaatil Gowerker; Satyankar
                                     Gowerker S/O
5. Name of the persons who   : Aarti Devi R/O Delhi, J &K
   identified the dead body   (Cook)
6. Apparent cause of death   : Murder
7. Place from where the dead   : Central Delhi
   body was recovered
8. Age & Sex   : 2- Male ; 2-Female
9. Injuries found on the dead   : No injuries found on any of
   body   the bodies.
10. Name of the I/O   : ASI Mustaq Ahmed
11. Name of the office Incharge : Inpsr. Paramjeet Singh
    of P/S   SHO P/S Daryaganj

11. Name of the office Incharge of P/S	: Inpsr. Paramjeet Singh SHO P/S Daryaganj
12. Name of the supervisory officer	: Dy. SP. Dewakar Singh SDPO Daryaganj.

Brief facts of the inquest proceedings are that on 07-09-2015, an information was received at P/S Daryaganj through reliable source to the effect that dead bodies of Rishi Gowerker S/O Satyankar Gowerker S/O Aaatil Gowerker; S/O S. Gowerker W/O S. Gowerker; R/O Central Delhi, and Babloo R/O Amroha, U.P. (Servant) were found at their residence. Since the death of deceased has occurred under suspicious circumstances, to ascertain the cause of death, nothing can be said until the medical reports come. Inquest proceedings U/S 174/Crpc has been initiated vide DDR No.04 dated 22-04-2015 at Police Station Daryaganj. The enquiries entrusted to ASI Mustaq Ahmed of Police Station Daryaganj.
Hence SR-A is submitted.

NO: 242/SDR
Dated: 07/9/2015

**Dy.Supdt.of Police,
SDPO Daryaganj**

Copy to:
1. Inspr. Gen. of Police JZ Daryaganj
2. Inspr. Gen. of Police C&R Daryaganj
3. Dy. Inspr. Gen. of Police ND Range Central Delhi
4. Sr. Supdt. of Police Daryaganj

> 5. Supdt. of Police Hqrs. Daryaganj
>   …….. for favour of kind information please.
> 6. SHO P/S Daryaganj for information and necessary action
>
> **SDPO Daryaganj**

So, this case was also a case where the family was brutally murdered by a scalpel. It was a level three murder.

If the murderer is the same for both the cases, he must be someone with some knowledge of medical science and pharmacology, Mathur said to himself. He knew from experience that using a scalpel on a human body was a tough job. The pain and the eye contact was something not everyone could withstand.

"The scalpel was used calmly over the arteries without any attempt of failure, draining all the blood out of the body. The three members of the family were killed. The bodies had been sent for postmortem. The reports were awaited." Mathur gave notes to Bhandey who curiously wrote everything on a sheet for the record.

"So what is the clue here, sir?" Bhandey asked curiously.

"The murderer left no clue and our men could not investigate well. We need time to look over the facts," he replied.

Mahi and Arjun

Mahi sat on the bench, crossed one leg over the other and relaxed, waiting for Arjun or any of his friends. Mahi repented the rejection. It was all of a sudden. The wait was long and she was impatient. She touched her head with the back of her hand.

It infuriated her to find she was sweating. Around fifteen minutes later, she saw Eshaan.

"Hey Eshaan, where is Arjun?"

Eshaan was surprised that Mahi was looking for Arjun. He remembered the last talk he had with Arjun when he was upset after being rejected by Mahi.

"Well, I don't know," he replied.

"Ah! I must be an idiot to ask you that; he must be busy doping," said Mahi sarcastically.

Eshaan felt very bad at the way Mahi had said that. He knew well that Arjun did not have a good reputation, but he wasn't entirely characterless.

"Well Mahi, that isn't true." Eshaan wanted to tell her where Arjun was. "He really likes you Mahi."

"You are saying this Eshaan, you? Who knows it well that your friend is a druggie and does not have much of a reputation," said Mahi.

"He really likes you; he told me," Eshaan stuck to his statement.

"He told you that," Mahi smirked. "I don't trust him. Honestly Eshaan, if it was someone else, I would have given him a chance. I mean, he is a nice guy but has bad habits." Mahi seemed to have a really bad impression of Arjun.

Ehsaan held Mahi's hand and took her to the other side of the campus.

"Come along with me," Eshaan took her to the rehabilitation section of the school. It was a psychological assessment and drug rehabilitation centre for drug addicts like Arjun. Since Shimla was a place where students were targeted more by the drug peddlers, the school had started this new initiative. Everything here was done in a controlled manner.

"Look here!"

He told her to look through the window of a room where Arjun was getting treated for drugs.

"Did he confess?" Mahi asked.

"Yes Mahi, he is doing everything for you because he wanted you to believe in his love for him in return. I hope you at least respect his feelings a little."

Eshaan left her there to ponder about what she had said a minute ago about Arjun.

Arjun was asleep on the bed in the room. Mahi felt guilty for everything she had said to Eshaan about Arjun.

Never thought someone will do something like this for me. Is his love real? Mahi asked herself. And she could not resist, so she stepped inside the room and went near the bed. Arjun opened his eyes to find Mahi in the room.

"Ah! Mahi. Good to see you. Well, I really want to be a good guy," he said though he did not want to disclose it at that moment. "I wanted to tell you this, but before that, I wanted to get a clean chit from here," he added. "I really adore you. Be with me Mahi?" he continued.

Mahi did not look up at him, fearing her eyes brimming with tears will not be able to hold them back for long. "Be with me," he pleaded and held her hand.

Mahi stood still. Suddenly she felt complete being there with Arjun. She was very impressed by the efforts made by him.

"I can give it a chance, but please don't believe this is love," Mahi said haltingly. "Just friends," she offered her hand.

"Friends!" Arjun smiled and shook hands as if he was sealing a pact.

Mahi and Arjun were friends now, and everything was going smooth. Arjun was trying too hard to make a place in her heart, and was successful at some level. Mahi had now started trusting him like never before and a time came when they both became best friends. Mahi then did not want to be in a relationship with Arjun whereas the want for love always remained in Arjun's heart. He always tried to make her feel that he was still waiting for her reply. Mahi always skipped it because she did not want to ruin their friendship. And then one day…

"Mahi." Arjun was a little far away so he waved his hand, but Mahi was busy over the phone.

As he reached close to her, before he could tap her shoulder, he heard her say, "Love you" on the phone to someone.

He remained silent and waited.

"Bye," Mahi put down the phone.

"Who was he?" Arjun asked angrily. "So this is the guy because of whom you are not accepting my proposal. I am such an idiot to love you like anything!" Arjun screamed in anger.

"Arjun…"

Before Mahi could say anything, he cut her short.

"You told me you are not ready for a relationship. If you're smart, you can make time to do anything. Busy is an excuse, not a reason. The real reason may be that a love interest is a 'distraction'. I can understand this if it was you working on something with looming deadlines like our final exams. I would have easily digested it, but watching you in someone else's arms…" Arjun screamed as Mahi was not giving him time and had been caught mouthing sweet love words to someone. This was something Arjun could never accept.

"But…" Mahi stammered.

"There's always a 'but'. Remember, this other person does not need to consume your being and all your time. I have to be there in that place... in your heart. I have the potential to be another facet of your life that could potentially enrich it beyond your wildest dreams, opening the door to new experiences, thoughts and feelings you never thought were possible," he continued a little quietly as Mahi had tears in her eyes.

"Who the hell is he?" Arjun took her mobile and broke it into pieces by throwing it over the wall. "Who was he?" he shouted again looking into her eyes and holding her arms roughly.

"My father," Mahi said quietly and Arjun's clutch loosened.

That night, Arjun texted Mahi.

I am sorry.

A message popped up on the screen of her broken phone.

What is it now Arjun? Mahi texted back.

I care for you, I love you and I can't see you with anyone else.

I really care. He texted these messages at the same time.

No reply came from Mahi and Arjun slept repenting his bad behaviour.

Early in the morning, as Arjun woke up, he saw a message flashing on his phone.

You always say I don't give you time... Let's go for a date.

Arjun smiled after reading Mahi's message. A bit of emotional blackmail never goes in vain. Heck, it works nine out of ten times.

Mahi was excited for their first date. She spent the entire morning dressing up. She was still confused about what to wear. There was a whole load of cashmere jumpers and a few dated ball gowns. She would probably keep them for the souvenirs of times in the past. One of them was her mother's eighties sari and a halter neck dress, A-lines deliciously visible, with a pattern that swept down the floor. Another was a floating chiffon one. Her wardrobe was full of shoes – silver, gold, mules, wedges, strappy sandals, boots, belts and bangles.

That evening, they visited the International Center for Science. There were a couple of exhibitions on which Arjun thought Mahi would be interested in as she was a studious student. He suggested to her to meet him there before dinner.

Mahi was also looking pretty in the dark blue Seven M&M denim jeans, tan colored ankle boots with a stiletto heel, a light colored DKNY top and a dark brown leather jacket. People around noticed them and complimented them with their stares. Arjun was very impressed. She was certainly a girl apart.

They chatted while they viewed the exhibits, then they took the little lane to a Japanese restaurant nearby for dinner. On the way in a lonely narrow dark street, Arjun offered her an electronic cigarette. It was his trick to check her confidence; he was way too smart. She took it and lit it. Then he looked into her eyes and asked for the same cigarette and she gave it to him. There was a smear of lipstick on it, and it gave an odd satisfaction to know her lips had touched the cigarette before his.

For the next ten minutes, they walked in silence. Arjun said, "Let's move in." It was one of his favourite restaurants. He loved sushi. She nodded and stepped in. Once seated, Arjun dug out a packet from his bag and gave it to Mahi.

"I'd been shopping at Rag & Bone, one of my favourite brands, and chose an outfit for you," Arjun said.

"Thank you for the lovely gift," Mahi replied.

The conversation between them began easily and he asked her how she liked Delhi and would she like to live there. Mahi was slowly developing a soft corner for Arjun.

"I've lied to you about something," Arjun steered the conversation to another point.

There was a look of slight apprehension on Mahi's face. He was sure she thought the worst at that moment.

"I lied about my feelings, the first time ever actually. I'm not only in love with you, but actually head over heels for you and want to spend the rest of my life with you."

"Oh, is that all? When you said you lied about something I thought it was going to be big. But this is a big thing too and I can't say anything before thinking," Mahi replied.

"And the other thing?" Arjun asked.

Arjun was a very confident man and a little pushy too. He had asked her this before on the phone and she had kept her cards close. She couldn't afford to let her man get under her skin, and that too so soon after meeting him.

She knew it well that she should not give her virginity easily to anyone until she's sure that he's sincere and he genuinely cared about her. They talked about how things had been in the past and now how fast they were moving. Arjun told Mahi about the women he had seen in the past and how he was quite sure that she was the one for him.

After finishing their dinner, they walked two blocks towards the hostel holding hands. Just before they crossed the street for the hostel, Arjun stopped and pulled Mahi close for a kiss. And very passionately with confidence, Arjun touched her lips which were soft. Mahi closed her eyes. Arjun wasting no time kissed her gently. Mahi felt like Goldilocks… it was just perfect!

She slowly pulled away from him and said, "Hmm, you're a good kisser."

She knew he wanted to be more physically intimate with her; it was very evident from his body language, the way he kissed and then looked into her eyes.

"Promise me you will never leave me?" Mahi asked.

"If I know what love is, it is because of you," Arjun replied and tried to kiss Mahi again. Mahi resisted.

"Bye!" she stopped him and walked towards the hostel.

Finally, after seeing each other a few times over several months, they were really comfortable with each other. They had now enjoyed kissing and touching each other, talking about sex in a casual sense and generally fooling around about it. Arjun liked to lick her ears, which drove her insane. He loved to tease her because she was now reacting. He was so playful, and couldn't stop kissing her, and the same was the case with Mahi. She was in love. She loved to be pampered this way. Being at ease with someone, being close, intimate and playful was new to her, so she surrendered herself to Arjun completely.

"It's my birthday on Monday," Arjun said smiling at Mahi, but Eshaan was confused, as he knew he was lying.

"Happy Birthday in advance," Mahi babbled excitedly. "So what are you going to do on the special day?" she asked.

"We are going to have a huge party at my friend's place." Arjun smiled again, alarming Eshaan about having a party at his place.

"He is a localite and has a villa here," he narrated the plan.

"Let's call everyone on Monday," Eshaan suggested.

"Yes, you're in charge of getting everyone to the villa."

"And I want a gift from you!" Arjun demanded her to be his possession.

"What? I am already yours," she said innocently.

"I want to be the man; your first man… " Arjun gave her a hint.

"I am not yet ready." Mahi tried to stop him and ended the conversation.

Then that night, Arjun called her up and they talked about the whole dynamic thing; how they see sex as an equal relationship that is built on very good communication, trust and respect. Arjun was very clever with such things. When Arjun had started demanding a physical relationship with her, Mahi had been reading various books and learning through websites over internet about the first timers to find out more about sex and the precautions which should be taken. Armed with knowledge, she finally decided to take their relationship to the next level for her partner.

"Okay Arjun, we will do it on your birthday, but do propose to me in front of everyone that day. You haven't proposed to me yet." Mahi gave him the permission.

CASE NO 242

A meeting was held and the case discussed further. Since they were short of clues, Mathur felt uncomfortable responding to his seniors. His head felt like exploding. He was going to lose it for sure and then time stood still – seconds turned to hours, minutes to days, and hours to weeks. Everything seemed to be confusing and he, showing a little concern to the sources which could be used to crack the case, submitted his inquest.

1. **Inquest vide DDR No.07 dated 23-09-2015, regarding the death of Gowerker Family R/O Central Delhi, Daryaganj.**

I have gone through the CD file and found that there is insufficient material as well as statement of deceased further for registration of case. The photographs placed in the file indicate some suspicion as they have inhaled some poisonous substance which creates more doubts and needs to be verified from the watchman as well as from the other sources. Before registration, case matter requires to be investigated thoroughly on the following points:

a) What were the places of death and the body position at the time of death?
b) Distance of workstation and residential complex and mode of drive?
c) Enquire from watchman whether the residence was locked/ open?
d) How many rooms were there in the residential complex? Who was present in which room at the time of death, enquiry be made from servant at what time they had left the room and behaviour of deceased on the day of death?
e) Telephone calls to be securitized in detail.
f) The CCTV camera footage of the house and places nearby.

The present I.O is directed to call neighbours and source persons to verify the above mentioned points and then go for registration of case.

NO: 242/SDR
Dated: 23/09/2015

Dy. Supdt. of Police
SDPO Daryaganj

Copy to:
1. Inspr. Gen. of Police JZ Daryaganj
2. Inspr. Gen. of Police C&R Daryaganj
3. Dy. Inspr. Gen. of Police ND Range Central Delhi
4. Sr. Supdt. of Police Daryaganj
5. Supdt. of Police Hqrs. Daryaganj
    …….. for favour of kind information please.
6. SHO P/S Daryaganj for information and necessary action.

SDPO Daryaganj

Mahi and Arjun

On the day of the house party, Chinese lanterns hung around the gardens, which was half decked and half lawn. There were loads of floating candles in the bowl of water, and large cushions were kept randomly. A special cocktail had been designed by a bartender friend, and there was a lot of good food on platters buffet-style with the usual dips, olives and salads.

Mahi was dressed in the white dress which Arjun had gifted to her on their date and she was looking like an angel.

"This way." Arjun showed her the way. He wrapped his arms protectively around her waist. His hair was black and shiny, and she was dressed more casually than usual. Everyone was present, it was a pool party. The cake arrived, the ceremony started. Everyone wished him whereas Arjun had something for her. He offered her a ring.

"Would you like to be my girlfriend?" he proposed to her publicly. The proposal was a romantic one, and nobody had expected anything like that from Arjun.

"Wow!" A girl from the back screamed at Arjun loudly.

Arjun smiled at her but Mahi kept looking at him lovingly, blushing.

"I am not ready," she said with embarrassment.

"Take it." Arjun took Mahi's hand and asked her to wear it. She knew it was a diamond and it felt like a burden. Nevertheless, she took it. It was his birthday and she did not want to hurt him.

"This way Mahi, we have other arrangements," he took her to the other room.

A table was placed in the center of the room with the champagne and ice, ready to be enjoyed.

"Arjun, please let's stay with everyone else. What will they think about us being alone in this room?" Mahi felt embarrassed being alone in the room with Arjun.

Arjun suddenly knelt on his knees and gave a rose to her. The romantic moment froze.

"Please Arjun," she pleaded.

"I really love you!" he said romantically. It was so heartfelt that Mahi could not refuse him.

"Look, I am wearing your ring," she showed him.

"You are mine," Arjun eyes beamed.

He then filled the two champagne glasses and offered it to Mahi.

"I've never had any." Mahi was reluctant to drink it.

"Trust me!" Arjun replied.

Mahi took the champagne from Arjun, and he smiled looking at her. Then he filled the glass again offering it to her. Mahi took it again. She then had another drink and a couple more. The drinks and its concentration was lethal. They crept up on her slowly, and like a sledgehammer, hit her hard.

"Let me show you the house," Arjun stood up.

"Sure." Mahi tried to stand, but her feet felt slow. The things around her started to move. Her breath felt heavy. She tried to balance herself but her vision seemed affected.

"Are you okay?" Arjun asked.

"Yeah," Mahi replied a bit unsteady. "Let's see the mansion," she continued.

Arjun took her towards the bedroom.

"Wow, this is beautiful!" she giggled, still struggling to keep her balance.

"This is the bed." Showing it, Arjun threw her hard on the bed.

"What are you doing Arjun?" Mahi asked.

"Nothing, just rest, you are not feeling okay." Mahi realized Arjun's intensions were not good.

Then Arjun too came over on the bed, unbuttoning his tuxedo.

"I love you," said Arjun coming close to Mahi.

Then he kissed her fervently... with love, with affection and tenderness. A soft kiss followed by a hard kiss, a kiss that made her so wet that it dripped down her inner thigh. Mahi stood up while kissing and started to walk outside the room, controlling her emotions.

"Will you be that girl?" Arjun asked passionately while holding her hand and not letting her go.

"Will you be the one to laugh with, talk to, and listen to, to hold and be held?" He then pulled Mahi towards himself. Keeping his arms around her, he carried her to the bed and Mahi wrapped her legs around his waist, ready to go along with the mad desire, a warm desire that could not be constrained any longer.

He kissed her again.

"Say something more," Mahi insisted, her voice was now sluggish. She was not in her senses and couldn't realize that Arjun was going to use her.

"Say you love me and tell me how much you love me," Mahi said, intoxicated.

"I want to watch a movie on the couch every day when I come back from work and end up on your lap entwined." Mahi kept telling him about her dreams and what she felt for Arjun while he was busy preparing to grab her.

"I want to feel your hand on the back of my neck, hold me with understanding, love and affection." Mahi gave him the way for more pleasure. She knew from here Arjun could not be stopped. Arjun patiently tied her by a rope and cuffed her before feeling her warm skin.

"Is this right Arjun?" Mahi asked while Arjun was busy undressing her. Arjun released her tension by massaging her breasts; and he was by then, hard.

"Will you be that girl?" Arjun asked again.

"Yes I will, I surrender myself to you Arjun."

Mahi was not feeling okay and her vision was more blurred by now. Arjun grabbed her and then kissed her on her tender tits. Mahi did not respond.

"Don't you love me?" Arjun asked.

"I don't know. I do, or maybe I don't. I am not sure," Mahi replied.

"Kiss me," Arjun suggested. Mahi started responding to him and they started kissing each other passionately. Mahi might be new to it, but Arjun was a player. He started undressing her quickly.

"What are you doing Arjun?" Mahi was uncomfortable.

"Trust me!" Trust was a word Arjun was good at breaking. Arjun undressed her. He left her hard and fondled her privates and went towards the wall. He was here to adjust the hidden camera whereas Mahi remained unaware of what was going on.

In the meantime, downstairs, the others had gathered around to see the action.

"Ladies and gentlemen, the show begins!" said Joy, the Italian friend of the V3 group, another heartthrob in the party as he switched on a 4K Ultra LED in the main room, inviting everyone to watch it. It was Arjun and Mahi's video being played live on the unit. Everyone in the room was shocked to see it and could not believe what they saw. Arjun was over the top, nude, throwing his passion over Mahi. They both were moaning to their fullest while the girls and boys present there enjoyed what was happening in the room.

Arjun teased Mahi with his rock-hard dick, rubbing the tip over her clitoris as she lay blindfolded on the bed, her beautiful taut nipples, her legs thrust apart by the rope, and her pussy glistening wet.

"I tell you what a beautiful, naughty, little slave you are! I tell you how hard you're making me, and how even though I like it, I'm going to punish you for it. I'll tell you how good you look, and how turned on I know that you are… and I tell you that you're totally at my mercy and that I'm going to tease you until you beg for me to make you come," Arjun said and laughed.

Mahi could not say anything. And then he thrust his hips forward and started to enter her mouth a little deeper. She moaned with delight... "Do you like that, slave?" Arjun asked.

"Mmmm..." Mahi moaned.

Her beautiful lips were wrapped around his manhood; her her mouth was wet and moist and warm. He pushed further in, his dick felt as if it would burst.

"Tell me how you love it!" Arjun exclaimed breathing faster.

Choked by lust and the dick, she managed to murmur, "I love it. I love your big hard dick... now leave me Arjun. We will do it some other day... I am not feeling well."

"Good girl! Would you like to be fucked now? Will you?" he asked, as he pushed further.

He eased off the rope a little.

"It's okay, you can do it, come on me Arjun!" Mahi gave him permission.

Arjun further made a move and bent slightly to reach the right place. "Take my dick, take it all the way..." He gave a thrust.

He slowly started to pump it in and out of her pussy, taking it a little further every time, filling her up, possessing her totally. She felt complete and amazed as her tight pussy constricted the entry.

"You are on the edge of the bed, come here." Arjun tried to set her for the camera angle. It was a clever move. Relinquishing control completely, trusting him, Mahi did as she was told.

"Push your limits, but keep it safe..." Mahi pleaded.

"Your pussy is like a river, the sight of your juices running down your thighs is almost too much for me to bear..." He withdrew his dick slowly. Mahi came for the first time and in front of the camera.

Arjun again made another move "Ah!" cried Mahi as he again started to fuck her.

"Please, it's too much!" she said, but watching her beg turned him on even more.

"What's too much?" he asked. He took Mahi's nipples in his mouth to make her hot again.

"Oh! Please!"

He released her swollen nipples.

"You look so beautiful naked!" Arjun smiled.

He then slowly and gently brushed his finger over the tip of her pussy. As he felt the warm breaths, he inserted his finger a little and almost got an orgasmic energy pulsed all the way down to her beautiful, wet, aching pussy.

Gently he sucked her nipple and her ecstasy built up. "Oh fuck!" Mahi moaned.

"Sure." Arjun make another move for the momentum.

"It feels so fucking good," Mahi cried in pain. "Fuck! Oh fuck me Arjun, so fucking good, make me come, please make me come…" she continued. Mahi came twice, anxiously being seduced by Arjun, and he threw his cum over her face with a wicked smile. He opened up the ropes, removed the blindfold and released her.

"Slut!" Arjun smiled and threw her clothes over her. "Wear them bitch!"

Mahi was confused hearing Arjun's words.

"Arjun?" she uttered softly.

"Yes, you slut… what did you think?" He looked at her with the glass in his hand.

"What did you say that day? You don't lose, and now you have lost everything to me." Arjun laughed. "Your virginity and your dignity," he said and continued sipping his drink.

"What are you saying?" Mahi felt like collapsing.

"Virginity in this room and dignity out of here in front of everyone." He gave an evil smile.

"Get out of this room, you bitch!" Arjun sat on the sofa and lit a cigarette.

"I hope you enjoyed being a porn star." He puffed out smiling.

Mahi wore her clothes, crying, and in no time, ran out from the place. It was a nightmare for her. She could not believe the friendship of all these months was just a ploy for revenge. This party was nothing but a plot. The trust she had in Arjun was just a lie.

As she opened the door of the room, everyone in the hall was waiting to see the porn star of the day.

"Hey Mahi, how much do you want for a night from me?" asked Joy making fun of her.

It was really horrendous to be so suddenly deserted. It came down to expectations, and Mahi was in tears. She could not stand there as her nude movie was still been enjoyed there in the hall by everyone. She ran towards the pool whereas Arjun too came out smiling. She threw the ring in the pool and looked at Arjun. He smiled as if nothing had happened. She was deeply hurt. She had no choice, so she jumped into the pool. She let the water pelt down, hoping it would somehow penetrate her skin and cleanse her.

Under a gray cloud that was her life, there came a silver lining – Eshaan, who had been an admirer of Mahi and knew she was right. He was now her friend too, so he jumped after her into the pool in order to rescue her. Arjun could not believe his revenge had taken such a bad turn. He stood there silently. In no time, Eshaan came up with Mahi in his strong arms; she had wanted to drown and die, but she was breathing. He pressed her stomach hard. Everyone was silently looking at both of them. With two gushes and water out from her mouth, Mahi regained consciousness. She said nothing. Eshaan gave her his tuxedo and they both went out of the house. Everybody left that day. Life had changed for all the people present there. Love was hurt and trust was broken. Mahi's MMS was on the card which everyone had enjoyed watching. Her nude body was news for the next few weeks. Eshaan the secret admirer was heartbroken; Arjun the culprit could not sleep. It was a sad end to a friendship and a love story.

What she really wanted to find was if there had been any love between them in the first place?

Case no 242

There was a panic in the city, with two murders and no arrests. There weren't even any leads as yet. The police tried to use their resources, but due to the pressure, most of the police services were halted. A covering letter was drafted then for the inquiry of the pending cases to SDPO Daryaganj by the Dy. Supdt. of Police as a regular routine.

The Inspr. Gen. of Police, No. 242/SDR.
JZ Central Delhi. Dated:- 12/9/2015.

Subject: **Follow up action on the instructions**
issued during the meeting held in ZPHQ
Central Delhi on 05/10/2015.

Sir,

Kindly refer to your office letter No.CRB/2015/13016 dated 11/09/2015 regarding the subject cited above.

In this connection, the requisite point wise reply is as under:

i)   Nil

ii)   I.   Case FIR No.35/2015 u/s 376/363/RPC, P/S Central Delhi .

II.   Case FIR No.56/2015 u/s 376/RPC, P/S Central Delhi.

III.   Case FIR No.53/2015 u/s 174/RPC, P/S Central Delhi.

IV.   Case FIR No.72/2015 u/s 376/363/511/34/RPC, P/S Daryaganj.

All the above mentioned cases are being closely supervised and necessary directions/guidelines were issued on spot to the SHOs as well as IOs.

iii)   Formal Inspections – nil
Casual Inspections – nil

iv)   03 PCPG meetings held in Delhi Metro Police point, Daryaganj.
(02 PCPG meetings conducted with SP Hqr. Central Delhi and 01 meeting conducted with SHO P/S Daryaganj.

Hence point wise reply submitted.

Yours faithfully,

Dy. Supdt. of Police,
SDPO Daryaganj

There was more pressure on Mathur due to which his eyes had sunk deep into his head. In nervousness, he lit a cigarette and leaned against the side of his chair. He took out his thumbed notebook and wrote the useful information regarding the case with the stub of a pencil. He did not look up as Bhandey came in to discuss and draft a follow up.

Sub Divisional Police Office, Daryaganj.

The Inspr. Gen. of Police, No. 242 /SDR.
JZ Central Delhi . Dated:- 25/09/2015.

Subject: Follow up action on the instructions issued during the meeting held in ZPHQ Central Delhi on 25-09-2015.

Sir,

Kindly refer to your office letter No.CRB/2015/13016 dated 25/09/2015 regarding the subject cited above.

In this connection, the requisite point wise reply is as under:

i)   03 casual crime meetings of important cases conducted by undersigned of below mentioned police stations

> ii) 04
> iii) Formal Inspections – nil
> Casual Inspections – 03
> iv) 03
>
> Hence point wise reply submitted.
>
> Yours faithfully,
>
> Dy. Supdt. of Police,
> SDPO Daryaganj

After drafting it, Bhandey left the room. Mathur sat back on his chair, concentrating harder on the case. He was not satisfied so he took out the photographs submitted by the Investigating Office and re-examined them. There was one photograph of the entrance to the crime scene which also gave brief details of the walls which were twenty feet high with cruel-looking steel barbs mounted along the top of it. One photograph detailed the furniture which looked very expensive. Nothing could remain unnoticed. Every possible clue was picked up along with the photographs of the dead bodies.

The scalpel was recovered from the garden with the blood stains on it. He knew that this was the only weapon used for the assassination of the Gowerker family, but he was still confused about how smartly a murderer could slit the wrists of each of the family members without getting caught and why did the other members not retaliate? It was obvious then that something might have been injected or given to them orally which made them unconscious, but what kind of drug it was had to be found out. He called Daisy to get information collected by the pathology department.

"Hello, this is Inspector Mathur again," he said.

"Yes sir, reporting," Daisy greeted.

"I want the report about the drug which had been used in the Gowerker case," Mathur asked for the report.

"Sir, our team of doctors have preformed the postmortem of few of the members of the Gowerker family and their report is yet to be submitted," she replied. "Let me do the paperwork from my office and get back to you," she continued.

Mathur sat back; he knew he would have to wait a while.

Things were not coming his way as expected. In nervousness, he put his hand into his pocket, took a cigarette, lit it, took a puff and let the smoke drift down his nostrils. Nicotine calmed him. He opened his little diary and noted down the facts and knots he needed to unravel.

Virat and Payal

Payal knew there was only one way she could win his heart, which was giving herself for the sake of her love. She knew the act of love would be a unique experience for him and he would enjoy her company. So she dressed in long pants, a white t-shirt and a light blue long sleeved over-shirt. It looked super sexy on her. They planned to meet at one of their friend's place. Karan came along with Virat.

Everyone stood silently in the balcony.

"Hi," Payal said to Virat. He also greeted her and Karan shook hands with her. Everyone seemed to be formal and for the next half an hour, they spoke very little and did not actually come to the point whether they were reconciling or not. Karan tried to broach the topic, but nothing seemed to help. Finally Payal asked the most vulnerable question. Karan knew this was the time that he should make himself scarce, so he bid adieu, leaving both of them alone.

"Tell me more about your new connections, and the girl you're seeing these days?"

"It's all very funny and this picture… it's the catalyst for a new connection between us. For me, it's more about being with this right person that I have found. To be honest, I still haven't found her myself. But there is something between me and the girl in this picture. Please don't judge me with my words or gestures, but keep me safe in your heart. I might have come across as rude sometime back, but I care for you!" Virat replied.

"To be honest, I would like a switch."

Virat confirmed that he was no longer interested in her.

"I was happy with you that you were dominant most of the times, and I know that sometimes I liked to be in control," Virat continued.

"I knew I never gave time to you Virat, but this time, I want to be with you and just you," Payal tried her luck.

"I love you Virat, and if it was just because I never get intimate or intense and that I was not open to a new experience, then I think I am ready for it too," Payal started unzipping her over-shirt in front of him.

"Please stop," Virat resisted.

He put a hand in his shirt pocket and dug out a picture which he carried with him all the time. "That's my girl," he told Payal.

Payal came close and tried to kiss Virat. Her hands moved down to his back and in return, not able to control the need that her touch aroused in him, Virat clasped her buttocks. She gave a long ecstatic sigh and her mouth found his. Suddenly the girl in the picture flashed in Virat's mind. He came into his senses. It was a sin for him to be indulging with someone else, so in anger, he threw Payal away on the bed.

"Stay away from me!" he shouted at her.

Payal felt cheap in giving her body to someone who did not want it. She had never felt so bad for herself. Both of them were in a rage and a loud argument followed between the two. Her face turned red and furious, she tore off her unzipped over-shirt and shouted, "I can give everything to you," and she served herself to him. Virat was still uninterested.

"It's something I'll never forget," Payal shouted back and zipped up her top. She was shattered from inside.

Virat could see the state she was in, and came and sat beside her. "Look Payal, you have to understand…," but she knew that Virat was crazy about that picture.

"I love you and will always do," Payal said, but Virat knew it was useless to make meaningless conversation, so he decided to leave.

"I don't care," Virat replied in anger.

"But…" Payal tried to communicate.

"You can't win all the time," he replied hitting his fist on the door while making an exit. Payal closed her eyes and concentrated more on what wrong she had done to the relationship, remembering everything he had said to her. The fear of Virat's love for the girl in the photograph that was gnawing at her had now ruined her life.

Mahi and Arjun

After the incident, Mahi left the school and went back to her hometown. She lodged an FIR against Arjun, Eshaan and Joy. But life was now hard for her family. Arjun sent Ehsaan to Mahi to reconcile, but she was very depressed. Her white face looked wooden, her eyes were swollen as if she had not slept for months and she trembled with fear. To break her confidence, Arjun's father used his political links to manipulate the case.

Moreover, he bribed the Investigating Officer who also changed the Doctoral MLC reports which clearly mentioned that no forceful sex was performed and that the sample of her urine also had alcohol and other toxic substances in it. When Mahi went to the doctor for help, he said she should quit, and he was pretty serious about it. But she didn't want to. Everyone talked about Mahi's MMS but she knew that this was the others' version of the story and the truth was completely different. Mahi did not lose hope.

To break her and to end the case, Arjun's father consulted his business partner and hired professional killers, who one day broke into Mahi's house, emptied the LPG cylinder, put some kerosene and flamed it up. The flame ran up a rag and into the kerosene tanks which were intentionally kept by them and an explosion took place. A blast of scorching air struck indicating the amount of thrush. Luckily her family members were not at home. Mahi could see the black smoke and huge orange- colored flame engulfing the whole area. She could feel the heat against her face. There was nothing her father could do. By the morning, the flame had died and smoke had cleared. Few parts of the house were still burning furiously, and heat was scorching. Mahi looked at the ruins of her house.

"We could have been inside…." her father said in fear. A creepy sensation crawled up her spine and this thought quickened her heartbeat.

But Mahi did not drop the case. She along with her family shifted to Delhi after the incident and tried to live a secret life there. Her father lost his business deals and reputation. Mahi lost her faith in the law that day when her father maintained a sulky silence towards her. Mahi was now just a burden on the family. She started to spend most of her time alone.

One day, the Investigating Officer from Shimla broke into Mahi's house in Delhi. Her new rented house was small with a few rooms. They were warm, but not completely furnished. There was a stale smell of cigarette smoke that made the officer wrinkle his nose.

"Give me ten minutes, either sit or you can leave, but I am here for your good," the Officer said and Mahi sat down to listen to him.

"Look, you already know whom you are fighting with. I would better suggest you to negotiate or you have other options too." He looked deep into her eyes.

"All right, girls with principles bore you. You find someone raped as a justified act. The people, for whom you came, may be right until the truth comes out. I would rather leave you with them," she said and stood up.

"I suspect you would rather slit your pretty throat then."

Mahi looked at him; she had already tried to commit suicide many a time, but the kind of education she had taken did not let her break down and she fought for her innocence.

"I think I will fight for my rights," she said boldly. And that was the last time someone from Arjun's side came for a negotiation. Since the families of all the three culprits were influential, she finally lost the case. Her last hope also vanished. She was now like a dead girl walking with no aim. She started to spend most of her times outside the house. She became a drunkard. Her father started to spy on her, and her trust in her family was broken. Her father had remained silent all these years, but one day…

The rain was pouring down and a light breeze flocked her curls slightly, the silent spectator of all that she had experienced. Soon the blood would stop flowing. So would the breeze.

With her fingertips, she enclosed the knob of the door. Icy to the touch, Mahi could almost feel the cold winds of death upon the house whose door the ex-inhabitant so foolishly had left open. It was almost as though she'd been invited in to join the voices just beyond the door. She twisted the knob, forcing the blood on her hands to stain the surface of the sphere and silently entered the house.

She stepped in; closing the door behind her and getting a better look of the area around. There was something like a hallway which had a door on each side. They led to the bathrooms. At the end of the hall was the living area, and hidden out of the view on the other side of the wall was a kitchen. To the left of the hall, leading out into the entrance where she stood, were the stairs that the two were sitting on.

She blinked. They'd whispered something inaudible to her ears and ran back up the stairs. She would have understood immediately, but her attention was drawn away by the sound of an older voice, which she recognized to be her Dad's. She'd thought about him previously.

She looked over at the man; he was about the same height as her. Mahi's dark glance was met by two cold grey eyes. The man repeated his question.

"Where were you?"

Mahi controlled herself back into that maddened grin. She made no vocal response, but simply shifted. She knew that her father suspected her of doing something.

"Daddy?" She looked at him with grief.

"Shut up, Mahi!" her father screamed.

"Everyone in the town is calling you a slut." It was the first time her dad was speaking to her in such a way.

"Don't tell me to shut up!" Mahi had no choice than to revolt, but she realized it was a waste of time to wait there anymore.

She returned the favour by kicking at the railing. "Wow! This is what I thought. Get out! Go to your room! Or go bug that bastard! Our relation is over!" her dad growled back, verbally abusive to his own child.

But this merciful gesture passed rather quickly, as she remembered she had to operate in a timely manner to avoid further detection; she needed to get it aborted. Mahi looked at her dad again.

Without saying a word, he stood tall, keeping his eyes upon his prey. He shrugged the cloak off a tad so his shoulders were free. He knew that this time, he'd have to use the other hand. The chainsaw gear shone in the ceiling lights and it reflected in his eyes; even for somebody so stupid, he was able to grasp the entirety of the situation.

She didn't care much as she knew that to end this unborn life was not so tough for her rich father. Satisfied, Mahi resumed her business downstairs. As soon as she was done, she treaded through the blood puddles in the hallway and up the stairs, staining the carpet with bloody footprints. She heard a few vaguely familiar voices as she walked to one side of the room. She heard the voice of the shuffling, and someone crying – they may have come to know of the mess, she figured.

She could hear her mother whimpering as her father growled in anger. "Why did we allow her to go to school? It is all because of your callousness!"

Her mother, now crying aloud shouted, "This girl! This girl has made me kneel in shame. God! She must have wooed those boys. These boys are from rich families. She is at fault for sure. I repent the day I gave birth to this slut!"

"I wish I could strangle her to death, only that I would be jailed. Or else…" Her father's voice trailed into a silent gasp of anger.

The rain was getting heavier; the blood was flowing out of the house through the drain, diluting itself into the rain-water. Maybe some bits of her would get evaporated along with the raindrops. Maybe then she would finally find peace.

"Where will we get a groom for her? Who would want to marry a polluted girl? What a shame she has put us all into! Even the most lame of boys ask for such a huge dowry. What do we do with her?" Mahi's father scuffled as he said those words, emotions searing through his chest, hot and burning.

He inhaled deeply. Standing against the window, the breeze touched his face and sent cool shivers down his spine. He closed his eyes for a moment. He saw Mahi, a little girl playing with a bowl, pretending to cook lunch for him. She looked at him, draped her chunni over her head and came running to him with the bowl filled with boiled rice.

"Baba, I cooked this! All by myself," she exclaimed as she proudly presented the bowl to him, her eyes twinkling. The twinkle seemed to dull slowly, until it blurred completely.

His eyes opened, and his hands reached out, as if to get hold of his little daughter. He sighed. That little daughter had proved him wrong. She wasn't that little anymore. In fact, it was unbearable for him to even call her his own! Mahi's father sighed, took in another deep breath and continued, "When a daughter is born, her marriage becomes a father's major concern. She becomes the upholder of the father's respect and dignity. When Mahi was born, I knew I have a burden to carry. But I never knew the weight of it until today. What face will I show to the society?

"She got herself raped! And that too, seen by the entire city! The MMS flooded so quickly over the internet! Sexually enticing whore! Thankfully, the police forgave her for filing the complaint in the police station and asked her to take back the case and let the issue die away quietly. Or else the surrounding people would have also come to know about this shameful incident!"

The sky had almost emptied itself, detached from the weight of the clouds that clung to it just hours back. The earth smelled of home; a place meant for all to exist but few to live. The rain had filled almost every hole, even the ones that hid themselves behind walls or creeks and beneath layers of silt. The sky was clear now, greeting a new morning. The rain had gone, so had the night. The night that promised darkness for some, to others, it was just another night to sleep.

Mahi's father looked across at the picturesque scene outside. It gave him hope, a silent nudge that things would get fine from here on. The horizon seemed distant and blurred, as if it challenged him to go forward and grasp it. It reminded him of the glance he had seen of his daughter the previous night. He walked down the corridor and entered her room. He found darkness looming in, as if it wished to engulf the room and everything it contained. His eyes struggled around the room, searching for her. And he stopped midway, as he saw her lying on the floor. Silent and lifeless.

She had found her peace, somewhere in that darkness. In the drops of rain that smothered the pain she had experienced. There would be no pain now and no shame too. It was never going to be an ordinary day in her life. It had taken in too much and given her what she finally needed the most: Peace. Justice had never been an option.

Case no 242

Due to the unsolved murder mystery, the law and order situation worsened in the city and people were in constant fear as none of the agencies had any clue about the psycho killer. A mob staged a protest and the situation became more volatile. To maintain safety, a curfew was imposed in a few parts of Delhi. People were told to stay inside their homes.

As Mathur entered the headquarters, he was handed over an order by the magistrate to work upon the safety of citizens in the city. This was very disappointing for him because he was already under pressure to solve the murders.

As Bhandey handed over the order to Mathur, he was disappointed to hear that he was given other things to handle when he was concentrating on the cases. He knew he was close to cracking them. The media was putting more pressure on the CID rather than the police.

But there was nothing that could stop Mathur from solving the case. Giving time to his team and deploying good counterparts to control the mob, he went to his station.

He settled down on his desk and opened the Case 242 file, going further through the case. As he saw the CID officer entering his office, he pretended to ignore him. Swaggering into the office, he thrust the papers down on Mathur's desk.

"Reports," said the CID officer, handing him pathological reports as he settled in Mathur's office.

Mathur ignored everything and cried out loud, "I don't believe you," and raised his gun towards him.

"We are in the same team." The CID officer pointed at the photograph.

"Look at this tree; this tree has the apples full of drugs."

"Each apple was sent to be tested," he continued.

"This murderer knew the family would eat apples from their royal garden farms."

"They have plenty of these trees, but still…"

"He injected this drug which he got from some place into each and waited for them to be eaten."

"Clever bastard!"

"They might have had a few before they became toxic."

"These are the reports of the local pathological laboratories."

"A murder committed very smartly."

"Look at this report." Mathur showed him the report about the bodies where the arteries had been slashed with the scalpel and blood drained on the floor. This was the report from the second case.

"How it was done?" he asked.

"Something was used because of which these fellows went into deep sleep. He could have intoxicated them, but he wanted them to die brutally."

"So what do you want to say?" the CID officer asked.

"Look, it is very clear that there is a link between these murders," he replied. "And you know what, we also know about the place where the next crime will take place," he continued. "He will go to kill another iron man of this city"

"Who?" asked the CID officer looked at Mathur.

"Sector 45, house no 24, David Turex. A former Italian and now an NRI," Mathur finished confidently.

They were still deep in thought over what Mathur had just revealed, when his phone rang.

"I think you are unable to handle this case and hence we will give this case to a new investigating officer. It will be better if you hand over the files to him; he is reaching the station. He has been especially appointed by the Delhi CMO," said the IG as Mathur picked up the call.

"I am very close to solving the case," Mathur replied, but the senior was not in a mood to listen to him. There was uproar and a great deal of heated conversation between them. And Mathur could not do anything else than withdraw from this case. Red-faced and furious, he tore off the pages in his hands.

"I am not a part of this case anymore." Mathur sat on his chair again, feeling low as he was so close to solving it. His mind went back to the past; the same things were again happening with him. He knew next he had a pending transfer. He sat down silently, opened his drawer and gave an envelope titled 'CID hunt at the office 1:30 p.m.' which had the video saved in the memory card to the CID officer who was listening to everything.

"The video of you spying in my office." Mathur said and the CID officer looked at him confused.

"I want this operation to be successful," Mathur said.

"Look, I owe you something then. We can still continue to work on this case till your orders come on the table," the CID officer gave him an idea. "What if we both go to Turex's house and give him the information in order to help him?" he continued.

Mahi and Arjun
Eight years later

Arjun knew that Mahi hated him. At the time of the incident, Arjun was young. He thought it was a joke, but now, as he grew older, he realized he was wrong. Every time he remembered the incident and that empty space created by Mahi, a cold chill of fear crawled over him. Every day he faced child-like-terror.

"You are burning yourself Arjun. Are you insane trying to search for someone who has not been heard of all these years? I will suggest to you to forgive and forget," said Joy to Arjun, consoling him. Eshaan was not Arjun's friend anymore. He sat on the large sofa, his eyes rounded as he listened to what Joy was saying. He kept on recalling the incident, facing the truth. He lit a cigarette between his nicotine-stained fingers, and his eyes glittered behind his spectacles.

"How can I?" he replied in the same monotonous stubborn tone. This was not for the first time they were talking about this incident.

"Are you still carrying it with you?" Joy questioned.

"Always!" He stared.

"Unbelievable!" Joy uttered surprisingly while maintaining eye contact.

"Joy, this is repentance. And there were times we were so wrong... Do you remember our techniques with women who did not cooperate with us?" Arjun asked.

"We believed women were easy. But you can't hope to run away and hide. Sooner or later, your conscience finds you."

"You know, there are two kinds of people. Those who walk along with the girl who they desire but do not get. When they don't, they splash acid on the girl's face. Her flesh peels off. The other kinds are those who'd grab the girl and shove her into their car and take her to some house. And then they'd brutally violate her so that she cannot walk with her head held high ever again. And you know what girls would prefer out of the two? The acid over the other treatment." He looked straight into Joy's eyes.

"You are playing with fire," Joy hated him for his decision to repent and scolded him like an elder brother.

"If you ever find her, do you think you can tie this knot of a relation which has no roots of truth? A relation that has given her nothing more than a painful end and god knows how many sleepless nights with tears that she must have shed on her pillow."

"I need to find her," Arjun said ending the conversation. Years passed by and Arjun kept himself busy with his father's pharmaceutical business in Delhi, trying to find the whereabouts of Mahi.

One fine day, which turned to be a life-changer for him, he got a friend request from a girl on Facebook.

Do you remember me?

It's me Angel from JKFY School.

Another message popped up after the unnoticed and un-replied message a few days later.

Who is this?

Arjun messaged back.

Arjun then spent a whole day going through her profile and her timeline for authentication. She was real and her name was the first thing that hit him. She was a Shimla boarding school's student. A few more messages and this conversation became more and more regular.

Can't you use your own pic as your DP? Arjun messaged her one day.

As this conversation continued from days to weeks and then months and as the relation blossomed, it shifted to Facebook chat and exchange of Arjun's number and address. One day over chat, Angel said something to Arjun.

Do you remember I used to be an innocent girl you made an MMS of? Do you remember the date; that Japanese restaurant where you asked to make out for the first time when I was a virgin?

You said you had a deep crush on me, and I eventually fell in love with you; trusted you for everything. . . but you ruined a loving heart.

"When I tried to get back to my life, I could not get rid of the memories of the incident anymore," Arjun cried out loud, for this was not Angel but Mahi messaging him. He asked for her phone number, but she logged off.

The same thing happened with Eshaan and Joy around the same time. Months passed chatting with the girl on Facebook and finally they too decided to exchange addresses and numbers. They tried to dial her number, but it was always switched off. Even her Facebook ID was deleted. None of the three could make any contact with Mahi thereafter.

Virat and Payal

It was difficult for Virat to waste any more time; he found himself trapped in her love. All he needed was to make a move because *one good turn deserves another,* so finally he decided to travel. Time travelled hard for Virat, as he knew more about this girl now; her address was in his hand and he wanted to go to Delhi to meet her.

He noted down the place where this girl lived according to the school records - Lajpat Nagar, Old Storey Building.

So, Lajpat Nagar was his destination. He took a bus as he knew nothing about the place; it was a pure concrete jungle.

After six hours, reaching ISBT by bus, he had reached the halfway mark to his destination. He first decided to get himself a room. He called a hostel friend who was a Delhiite.

"What! Are you insane? You travelled on your own?" he scolded.

"I want a solution," Virat replied bluntly, wasting no time. "If you can arrange an accommodation, let me know," he continued.

"Okay, give me an hour. I will try to get you a place."

Virat crossed the road and went to the other end. It started to rain heavily. He was all wet but his spirits were high. He decided to take an auto rickshaw to his destination.

"Where do you want to go exactly in Lajpat Nagar?" asked the driver.

"Old Storey near Moolchand bridge," Virat replied him confidently as though he knew the place.

"A hundred rupees for it," the auto rickshaw driver confirmed the fare.

"Okay!" he agreed.

It was early in the morning, so the streets of Delhi were comparatively quiet. Everyone was enjoying the summer rain, except him.

"You are under Moolchand; should I take you to the central market or the other end?"

"The other end!" Virat knew nothing of the place; it was just a hit and trial.

"Here we are, so where next? Should I drop you here?" the driver asked.

"Well, take me to the fourth block." He told him about the building he had to go to.

"Here sir, this is it," the auto driver told him.

He started to read the house number on every building.

"24 – F".

Finally Virat had arrived at his destination.

"Hello!" said Virat's friend after dialing his number.

"Hi," he replied.

"Who's this?" Virat asked.

"Idiot it's me; I have made arrangements for you. I will message you the address. You go there and take the name J.P. Nadda," he said.

And the phone call ended. Now Virat had to make a start. He was now at the destination.

Virat stood at the door and slowly pressed the doorbell. He then wondered what he would say.

"Yes?" A servant opened the door.

"Can I meet Miss Mittal?" Virat asked as he read the name on the name plate of the house.

"Memsaab, someone has come to meet you," she shouted loudly.

"What's your name?" she asked.

"Virat; actually she doesn't know me… I am from a Shimla school," he gave his introduction.

"Someone from Shimla," she again shouted.

"Yes?" Suddenly the girl came out. It was her! Virat's search, his love and his destiny.

Virat was happy and felt like he had traveled all the way for his angel. Yes, she was looking like an angel, but older. Olive skin, dark hair, in her twenties with twinkling eyes. She was dressed in plain white. He guessed her husband had passed away. She broke the silence.

"What do you want?" she asked.

"Miss, I am from the same school where you had studied."

"No, I never studied in Shimla," she retorted harshly.

"But…" before Virat could say anything, this girl tried to close the door.

"Please listen to me… I don't know what has happened?… why everyone is so weird about you." Virat tried to complete his sentence, but she turned around. The maid closed the door.

"This is your picture!" Virat took the torn out page with her picture out from his pocket and showed it to her from the window. She looked back.

"Please?" he pleaded.

"Should I call the police?" she shouted through the closed door angrily.

"Can you please listen to me for a minute?" Virat pleaded again. "I have come to Delhi for you," he continued.

"Why?" she replied back, her voice was flat and steady.

"I want to speak to you; can you help me please?" Virat asked.

She opened the door and leaned against it, giving him no way to pass. "I can't help you much. Why did you travel so far?" she asked being clear that she won't be of any help.

"I travelled for you. I can't stand the pain. I wanted to meet you." Virat's body was shaking; he stared at her with his small eyes.

"Sorry, what pain?" the girl asked. "This is no time to discuss all this bull shit," she continued. Virat smelt trouble. She was emotionless, and this made Virat sweat.

"I know something had happened and believe me..." Before Virat could convince her, she closed the door again. He got the answer sooner than he expected it.

He sat frozen, white-faced. He knew it was the last chance he had. He wrote his number with a message – *My love for you can't stop me from meeting you. I am here till the night* – behind the torn page with the picture which he had found in the annual book. He pushed it through the slit under the door and left.

Maybe she'll make up her mind to meet me once, he said to himself.

He walked alone along the road. He decided that whatever it took, he would convince her to believe him that he really loved her and he wanted her to be back on track, forgetting whatever had happened

A message suddenly popped up. It was from her.

I will meet you in half an hour at Okhla Market. The address of the meeting place followed.

Okay! I will wait, Virat typed back and boarded the bus.

He took the ticket and went to one of the last seats. The bus was full. For a moment he thought people were staring at him, but in reality, no one paid any attention to this average looking guy. It took half an hour for him to reach the desired destination. He rode all the way in silence.

"Okhla!" the bus conductor shouted. He stood up and went towards the exit. He felt a surge of blood move through him. A minute's walk and he would reach the decided place. He kept waiting near the gate for an hour. His legs were aching and he felt like blood draining through his legs, but this couldn't stop him from meeting her.

Finally, he saw Miss Mittal coming. She came close and sat down. Virat could hardly make eye contact with her. He knew something wrong had happened, but he was here to make things right. And the way she came inside, he knew deep within that it would not work. There was something stern about her. It was just that she did not want to have a real conversation. She shook hands with him, but his body was numb. He could barely say anything at that time. She took him inside the coffee shop. Her face wore a long-suffering look.

What will I say and from where will I begin? These things kept spinning in his head. They took their seats and an uncomfortable silence prevailed.

"Well, to start with, I got this picture of yours from the school library and since that day I started to search for you…" it was like his tongue was buried in snow, he could not even feel it. "I saw your name removed from the register and nobody was willing to talk about you," he said slowly.

"Well, let me tell you the truth then…" she interrupted him and she started narrating the story. She remembered the incident vividly. Her words made a tremendous impression on him.

Case no 242

They knew the link was in this place where they were headed together this time. As the CID officer along with Mathur entered House no 45, he was sure during these hours no one would open the door for them. They hid behind the wall, tried to peep in, but there were no guards. They hesitated as they tried to look inside the house, but the lights were dim. Mathur saw a flickering shadow moving. They looked at each other. Mathur raised his eyebrows once to ask the CID officer what to do.

"Move in," he whispered looking for his 0.4mm pistol. They climbed the wall one by one. Mathur then put his pistol down as he saw everything clearly. Both of them stood there for sometime, hiding themselves behind a tree. They waited for any further movement and when they confirmed everything to be clear, Mathur gave a signal to the CID officer to move inside the house.

Inspector Mathur took charge again and he took his gun in his hand to give him cover. Covering each other, they entered the house. The door was unlocked so it was not tough for them to break in; the ambience was silent, but disturbing. It was clear that something had happened over here. To find what had happened was the next thing to do. Both of them then tiptoed through the porch and entered one of the rooms.

They walked slowly up the broad staircase to the second floor. A long walk down a corridor lined on either side by medieval battle weapons brought them to a suite which consisted of a bedroom and a vast sitting-room. They let themselves into the suite and locked the door. The room was vast and wooden beams supported the arch of the ceiling. The big painting on the wall looked magnificent. The moonlight shone through the curtains making a pattern on the carpet. But the stuff in the room was all messed up like some fight had taken place. They were now sure about the murderer's presence in the house.

"Where now?" the CID officer asked Mathur.

"Bathroom." Mathur pointed at the door which was still a little opened.

His bravery fairly shattered, two steps forward, one step back, seemed like he was inching his way down a hot coal-laden path. A change of direction was required. As they entered the bathroom, it was all dark. Mathur searched for the switch and he turned on the light.

 "Holy shit!" uttered Mathur looking at the sight and he fell back with fear. Mr Turex's face and his head were brutally strapped. His brain was on the floor along with his tongue. The grimace on his face was intact and indicated a slow painful death.

Mathur took hold of his hand to check the pulse.

"Pulse is gone," he uttered and showing him the way out, suddenly a loud cry came from the other side of the house. They moved fast and travelled to the other side. Running on the way, he drew from his shoulder a Mauser 7.63 pistol, fitted with a silencer; he knew firing would be necessary. With a kick, they broke down the room's door.

Mathur's mind was flooded, rewinding through the old footage of the crime scenes in his mind. His emotions could work so fast and so well that he could go from white rage to placid blue in a mono second flat. It was draining. It was the slowest moving second of the word. The axe glittering in the light swung and there was a crutching sound of the blade crushing a head.

"Hands up!" said the CID officer in his husky voice, commanding in anger.

But the murderer kept hacking the body, almost as if he was doing it unconsciously. In slow motion, he inched his way directly towards the head, his pudgy fingers adorned with an axe. His mouth wide open, swear words cascading forth, and everything continuing on its own. He felt tired.

"Up I said!" shouted Mathur this time.

The murderer kept on hacking the body into pieces and then threw the axe aside, which made a loud noise. Everything came to a standstill, as if he had fled his own skin and spirit. The shock was subsiding and the realization rose of how vulnerable he was. He was still looking at the other side, with his back to both the officers. So, to get a vision of him Mathur ordered him to turn.

"Keep your hands on your head and turn around."

He obeyed obediently. He was young and short. A murderer who looked innocent.

As he turned back, they were shocked to see the face of the murderer. He was a young teenage kid. The blood stains were all over his face, racked by such destructive feelings and encouraged by his confidence. He was Virat!

"You are under arrest," said Inspector Mathur getting hold of him. Virat was handcuffed; his face was covered with a piece of cloth as he was taken away.

"Look down and do not look at the camera as we move out of this building," Mathur said to him in a threatening tone. "The media will be looking for you," he added.

And in no time, media gathered for the breaking news of the country.

The news flashed on the TV sets: *A seventeen-year-old kid strapped Mr Turex, his son, and is believed to be behind the other murders in the city.*

Case no 242 was closed now, witnesses were brought, evidence was taken, finger prints were recovered from door knobs and the axe. The kid had been charged with murder and was now in custody, awaiting further trial in the court.

Case no 242

Mathur filed the last report of the case as under…

SR-A Police Station Daryaganj. District Central Delhi.

Subject: - Inquest proceedings U/S 174/Crpc into the death of David Turex S/O Redgit Turex;   Joy Turex S/O David Turex, R/O Central Delhi.
District Central Delhi, initiated vide DDR No.06 dated 02-11-2015, P/S Daryaganj.

1.	Name of the person who lodged the report	: Police Station Daryaganj.
2.	Date of occurrence.	: 02-11-2015.
3.	Date of report and time	: 02-11-2015.
4.	Name of the deceased with full particulars	: David Turex S/O Redgit Turex; Joy Turex S/O David Turex, R/O Central Delhi
5.	Name of the persons who identified the dead body	: Dipanker (CID officer belt no 2446)

---

6. Apparent cause of death	:	Murder (Hacked)
7. Place from where the dead body was recovered	:	Central Delhi
8. Age & Sex	:	2-Male; 0-Female.
9. Injuries found on the dead body	:	Hacked brutally by an axe twenty times.
10. Name of the I/O	:	ASI Mustaq Ahmed
11. Name of the office Incharge of P/S	:	Inpsr. Paramjeet Singh SHO P/S Daryaganj
12. Name of the supervisory officer	:	Dy. SP. Dewakar Singh SDPO Daryaganj

Brief facts of the inquest proceedings are that on 02-11-2015, an information was received at P/S Daryaganj through the I/O and CID offier Dipanker on the spot found the dead body of David Turex S/O Redgit Turex; Joy Turex S/O David Turex R/O Central Delhi were found dead at their residence. Since the death of deceased has occurred in front of CID officer and the inspector in charge, case will be filed when the medical reports comes. Inquest proceedings U/S 174/Crpc has been initiated vide DDR No.04 dated 02-11-2015 at Police Station Daryaganj. The enquiries entrusted to ASI Mustaq Ahmed of Police Station Daryaganj.

Hence SR-A is submitted.

NO: 242/SDR
Dated: 02-11-2015

**Dy. Supdt. of Police,
SDPO Daryaganj**

Copy to:
1. Inspr. Gen. of Police JZ Daryaganj
2. Inspr. Gen. of Police C&R Daryaganj
3. Dy. Inspr. Gen. of Police ND Range Central Delhi
4. Sr. Supdt. of Police Daryaganj
5. Supdt. of Police Hqrs. Daryaganj.
   …….. for favour of kind information please.
6. SHO P/S Daryaganj for information and necessary action.

SDPO Daryaganj

Filing the case

With the investigation, they came to know that all the three gruesome murders had been committed by Virat. Now they wanted to concentrate more on the subject and under what bent of mind did he perform them.

To draft the case, they needed to know more about the case and the way the murders were committed. Mathur was also very keen to know how this little boy had managed to commit such a crime, so he went for the interrogation.

It was a big room with a table placed in the centre, bearing no other furniture. There was just a clock with a steady swing of the pendulum; the lead weight slightly touched the case of the clock, making a distinct regular noise. To the one side of the room, there was a hidden CCTV camera to record the interrogation.

"So if you will answer my questions and take me seriously, I won't be doing an interrogation," he said in a loud voice.

Virat barely moved, so Mathur continued, "So what do you have to say about using the chemicals for apples?"

Mathur always believed himself to be very patient, but this case had been the longest endurance test he ever had. It had taught him that if you wait long enough, and you were patient enough, you can fix what you are hired for. He knew sooner or later he would break his silence.

"Look, we know something was used for coating the apples," Mathur added.

He paused for a moment, and then went on, "What was that and how did you manage to do it?" He tapped with his fingers on the table, making the atmosphere more intense and looked at him, with anger. He tapped with irregular intervals.

Tap-tap-tap.

A long pause and then tap-tap.

But Virat did not say anything. Minutes dragged by. The pendulum of the clock continued with its soft irritating sound. Mathur was amazed at the way he had performed the act and killed the Singhals, but he was really very confused how he had managed to kill with the scalpel.

"Tell me what you used for killing the Gowerkers? How did they fall asleep?"

He slapped Virat. He knew he was confessing everything as well as helping to solve the case, but he could not resist his hands.

"Sir, I used Phospogene," Virat replied.

"What is that?" Mathur was not used to such terms.

"Sir, it is a gas that was used in the world war for killing the masses… it has an aphaxia effect!" he replied.

"How did you manage to get it?" It was an obvious question to be asked at this point. "How did you get them all together in the room and made them inhale it?"

"Well, the gas I used was Chlorine." Virat started to explain. "Chlorine is a simple compound and it is colorless as well as odorless. They were the reasons I chose this gas for the execution," he unveiled the whole series of incidents.

"I kept waiting for a chance to murder them. I knew very well that Gowerkers would definitely get the AC cleaned this summer. So I went to their home pretending to be from the AC company and I managed to install the chlorine cylinder there as a cleaning agent," Virat elaborated.

"Then?" Mathur was curious to know how a teenager could turn into a serial killer.

"I managed to add Chlorine gas from the cylinder into the gas kit and I used the vent of the normal Freon gas used for cooling," Virat detailed. "I replaced the gas with Chlorine and left a leakage which was not easily detectable, but also replaced it in such a way that only when the AC would be used the leakage will increase."

Mathur was stunned at the way Virat had planned it. "This is known as Britholite Poisioning," Virat added.

"How did you manage to get these cylinders?" Mathur wanted to know every detail. "Sir, first I tried to make this gas on my own by using Hypochloric Bleach with acid for producing chlorine gas, but it is unstable and it is difficult to concentrate at home or even in a laboratory. The calculation was simple: $NaClO + HCl$ and you will get Chlorine," Virat narrated. "But then I used the simpler way, I searched some underground selling website to get myself a container of this gas as it is used for industrial purposes."

"Bloody murderer!" Mathur shouted as he slapped him hard with a cruel grin on his face. Then in anger, he swung a surprising sucker punch on his chest, which threw him on the ground. Mathur stepped back while Virat struggled to get breath back into his tortured lungs. It took some time for him to recover from the impact of the punch.

Drafting the case

Before the Hight Court Sub Office Delhi.
In the matter of: SHO Daryaganj Chowki Central Delhi inquest for the proceeding of the murder trial

Esteemed/Sir,

May it please in your honour:-

The respondent most respectfully submitted the Para wise inquest preceding of Case no 242; reply by Daryaganj Chowki Central Delhi are as under:-

1. That it is a fact that the complainant belongs to the murder of Mr Turex and his family, Mr Gowerker and his family and Mr Singhal and his family, in the sequence; R/O Daryaganj Distt. Delhi.

2. That it is a fact that all the murders have been performed cleverly by a juvenile and there were hardly any eye witnesses to the murders. Later in the investigation I/O Mathur found that Virat who is the main accused of all the three cases of the said renowned families, police is unable to investigate further because of the human right commission for juveniles. Thus it is a request that special permission should be given to the department for the same so that further investigation could be performed on the basis of the collected samples.

3. Since the guilty has confessed his guilt, it is a request to the court to let the department seek this case under special case

act and the provision for the death penalty could be appealed by the government lawyer.

Annexure of above mentioned paragraphs enclosed for reference i.e
i)   Reports submitted by Mr Mathur- ANNEXURE-A.
ii) Reports submitted by CID officer at ANNEXURE A-1.
iii) Details and residential proofs of Virat and his school files ANNEXURE A-2.

As per Annexure produced, CID officer who was not at the time of the duty but was present at the place of crime becomes the eye witness and knocked the door of Hon'ble court and directed to SHO P/S Main Metro Police Station in terms of section of 304(A) Cr.P.C for registeration of case U/S 302/467/120-A/RPC against Virat. In compliance to court orders, the case was registered under FIR No.27/2015 U/S 302/467/120-A/RPC. The case is under investigation with P/S Delhi Hight court now to be shifted to fast track court.

(Photo copy of court order enclosed for reference at ANNEXURE-3.)

(Photo copy of FIR enclosed for reference at ANNEXURE-4.)

4.   That a complaint against Virat was received in this office from SHO Daryagang Delhi. The photocopy of the complaint enclosed at ANNEXURE for reference.

The contents of the complaint was that the on 02-11-2015, an information received at P/S Daryaganj through the I/O and CID offier Dipanker on the spot found the dead body of David Turex S/O Redgit Turex; Joy Turex S/O David R/O Central Delhi were found dead at their residence. Since the death of deceased has occurred in front of CID officer and the inspector in charge, the case will be filed when the medical reports comes. Inquest proceedings U/S 302/Crpc has been initiated vide DDR No.04 dated 22-04-2015 at Police Station Daryaganj. The enquiries entrusted to ASI Mustaq Ahmed of Police Station Daryaganj.

Since the matter was important in nature and the Senior Officers was apprised about the facts vide this office No.833-35/SDR dated 07-11-2015. The photocopy is enclosed for reference at ANNEXURE.

5. Adding to the annexure, the government infrastructure been thrashed by the people are residing in Sub Division Daryaganj who were affected by the violence due to this case. People are being given due redressal for their grievances. Therefore, the allegations on SHO Daryaganj are fabricated.

Recently in the same matter, when the accused person did not pay the dues to the Government Treasure Department. To which Treasury Office knocked the door of the Hon'ble court. The Hon'ble court has directed u/s 156(3) to register the case under relevant sections of law. Accordingly the case was registered under FIR No.28/2015 U/S 302/467/120-A/RPC P/S Main Metro Police Station. The photocopy of FIR at ANNEXURE and photocopy of complaint provided at ANNEXURE. The case is under investigation in which arrest of accused is certain.

The photocopy of complaint and receipt of payment enclosed for reference at ANNEXURE.

It is therefore humbly requested that the proceeding initiated against respondent i.e SDPO and SHO P/S Daryaganj be dropped.

Hence para wise reply is submitted.

Yours faithfully,

Dy. Supdt. of Police,
SDPO Daryaganj

"*Day 1 of the trial, three innocent families, brutally killed…*" The new flashed on TV screens.

And the interview was conducted overnight:

"Before we move further with the case, let's see the footage we have from the sealed house where the three incidents took place," said the reporter standing in front of the gate of the house, pointing towards the house.

"This is the place where Mr. Turex an Italian NRI was killed brutally…" she continued.

"So here with me is Mr Rajesh Patel, from the neighborhood where this incident took place."

"So sir, what kind of person was Mr Turex?" she asked.

"Well, he was a very kind-hearted person, we never talked with him much as he was always busy with his work."

"Did you ever see any kind of behavioral changes or any suspicious activity in the house?" Reporter asked.

"Never ever!"The neighbour replied.

"Let's move back to the studio."

At the studio, the news reader connected with Mathur over the phone.

"We have here on the line, Inspector Mathur, the investigating officer who solved this case with diligence. It was the most politically influenced case in the country," the news reader introduced the caller and quoted.

"Before we move further, we want to ask Mr Mathur, who actually is the serial killer?" Inspector Mathur was questioned on national news.

"Well, we are investigating this case further to find out the identity of this teenage kid and the link between all the cases."

"But I would like to mention here, case no. 242 is closed for trials, thank you!"

"What we have here is the picture of the teenage kid – the murderer!" They just flashed the picture around the country.

Trial Day 1:
In the court

"Submitting along with the Case file no 242 with other documents to represent the case, I Mr Devang will lead the case against the suspect Mr Virat." The government lawyer took charge of the case for the first proceedings.

Mr Devang was a sixty-year-old solicitor, a well-mannered, well-turned-out gentleman. He had a clear cut job since far. Whereas Mr Bishnoi was nowhere close to Devang, he did not look capable enough too.

"From Virat's end, I, Mr Bishnoi will lead the case," said the criminal lawyer to represent himself.

Mr Devang submitted the case file to the judge.

After receiving the first documents of the report on case no 242, the judges gave time for the next hearing and the court was adjourned for a week.

Trial day 2:

Everyone was present in the court. This time Virat's father also came for the hearing. He was shattered after hearing the news which had flooded the TV channels about his son and family.

"Kindly proceed with the case."

"After studying the file submitted to the panel of judges by Mr Devang, we give time to the opposition lawyer to give his opinion and what he has to say." One of the judges started the trial.

"Sir, I want to cross-examine the reports submitted by Inspector Mathur and the CID officer's allegations against my client," he asked for the grant.

"Granted, kindly submit one copy of the file to the opposition lawyer for cross examination," said one of the judges.

"Anything else you want to say?" and he asked Mr Devang to continue the proceedings.

Mr Bishnoi looked unprepared, for the court trial seemed unenthusiastic since there was an eye witness to the case and a confession which made the case solely one-sided.

"Sir, here I want to add few more medical reports and a CCTV camera footage of Mr Virat at the car parking and certain other places that prove he was present in Delhi at the time when these crimes took place," said Mr Devang, building a strong case.

And the trial continued where Mr Bishnoi seemed to be losing and Mr Devang took no time to sweep the case. Still the judges did not want to be very quick about their decision, so they gave some time to Mr Bishnoi so that more aspects of the case could be unfolded.

And the day ended with another proceeding to the case.

That evening at the Remand home

Virat's father went to the jail where he was kept. He wore a black dark tweed suit with an impeccable cut; over his arm he carried a bag, and a large diamond set in a heavy gold ring glittered on his thick little finger. He exuded money, power and luxury, but he did not look as good as he was. His hair had turned white due to less sleep. He had grown a beard. Sitting in the waiting room, he looked at the stuff kept there.

"I told you to control your anger," his father shouted and cried aloud as soon as he saw his son. "Do you even know how I had to beg to the MP for your freedom. I don't know where will this go and how I can help you," he said as they sat down.

"I don't care,"Virat said and started looking outside.

"Huh! Aren't you ashamed of your deeds?"Virat's father was ashamed of his son. "Thank god your mother is dead," he said in disgrace.

"You killed my mother!"Virat retaliated in anger and shouted at his father.

"What the fuck are you saying Virat? Are you insane or have you gone mad?"Virat's father said in a rage.

"You were busy with your secretary and other stuff when my mother was on her death bed. She needed you at that time the most, but you were unavailable. You never cared for us. Money was your only priority!"Virat said everything in one breath.

Virat's father knew what he was talking about. He knew it was the pain he had buried deep in himself long back when he was a child, much before he was sent to the boarding school.

"What did I not do for your comfort?" Virat's father asked. He knew he was wrong, but somewhere he had been a good father too. He had tried giving Virat a good education in comfort.

"I am here now to save you, but I don't think I can do it, since you have confessed. I don't even know why you have killed so many innocent people!"

"Innocent? Huh!" Virat replied.

"I love you son, you are my only asset." Virat's father hugged him hard. "And now this is how you repay your father?" He added as Virat did not hug him back and the time for the meeting in the jail ended.

Months passed after the witnesses had been examined and cross examined over the evidence presented in the court. It was almost clear that Virat was now close to be declared guilty. The trial was almost over, but due to his father's efforts, Virat was given time to represent himself. But nothing worked out for Virat, and all the efforts went in vain.

Trial day 18:

"In today's trial, I hereby want to present the lab reports concerned with the mysterious death of the Singhals. The murder was actually plotted by Virat with cyanide," said Mr Devang to the court. To which the opposition remained quiet. Mr Bishnoi knew there was nothing he could do to save his client. He now concentrated on his efforts to save him from a death penalty.

"Sir, this is the report," and he handed over the report to the panel.

In case no 242 further evidence has been collected from the bin which includes:
Cotton swabs – 2 in nos.
Vegetable peels
Apples – 6 in nos.

"All the evidences were submitted to the pathologist for the test and the reports said that there was a cyanide polish over the peels," Mr Devang tried to make the case stronger.

"Here I am submitting the details and the CCTV footage of Mr Virat while he went to the other part of the city to buy the stuff," he added.

"And adding to it here, in case no 242 part where Mr Virat used a certain gas in the AC vent. We collected the evidence as:

A.C. gas kit – 1 in nos.

A.C. pipes

And fingerprints from door knob - 3 in nos.

"All the evidence was submitted to the pathologist for the test and it matched exactly with Mr Virat, which showed his presence in Mr Gowerker's house." Mr Devang was fully prepared for the case.

"Here I am submitting the details of the lab reports of the fingerprints and also that Mr Virat worked as the technician for this AC vent cleaning company and went there to check the AC," and he handed over another report. Mr Bishnoi remained quiet. He knew the case was slipping away from his hands.

"Sir, I need to cross-examine the investigation done by the I/O. My lawyer friend forgot to share the evidence he was working upon with me, to which I cannot say anything right now," Mr Bishnoi played smartly to get time for the case as it was getting more complicated.

"The court is adjourned for the next hearing and we would suggest Mr Bishnoi to kindly come with the cross-examination."

And a few more weeks passed with the investigation and cross-examination. Due to the complications and since the culprit was a juvenile, there was a peer pressure over the panel too; the fast track court took fast hearings for the same.

Trial day 23:

After the series of tiring hearing trials, the court members and the panel of judges were confused about Virat being so aggressive. And the court, before giving the long-awaited judgment, compelled Virat to confess the missing link.

"What happened was totally expected when you commit a crime; you will get arrested and will go to jail. You should have known that," said one of the judges in anger.

"I would not have given him a death sentence, but the thing is, he is not even saying anything to tell us what is the connection of these people with him," he continued.

"You killed these three innocent families," shouted another judge.

"Brutally!" added the third.

"Yes, I killed all these families but they were not innocent." Virat for the first time said something in the court after three months of trial. He knew this was the final day and from here, things would change for him. He knew he would be punished for the crimes he had committed.

"Look at his face, he is not feeling ashamed to talk like this," one of the people present at the court said. There was media gathering in the court, waiting for the judgement.

"Tell us why you killed all these people?" asked one of the judges from the panel.

"Few years back…" Virat started narrating. "…There was a girl. Sweet and innocent… she had some dreams. Just like a cocoon ready to turn into a butterfly to explore this sky, who wanted to study and join her father's business. And for this, she studied day and night and got admission in a prestigious school. But she did not know that the prestigious school in Shimla would lead to her doom. Her new life started from there. A life full of love, emotions, anger, which knocked down this cocoon before she could turn into a butterfly. There she committed the biggest sin of her life. She fell in love with the wrong guy. She was connected to this guy, who subtly mixed her drink with alcohol in a house party which was a sweet trap for her. Into the delirium, she was forced to have sex with him. And this group of guys who were very influential in the school, made an MMS and flooded it over the internet." Virat confessed everything in front of the judges.

"Her life was shattered then. She could not do anything against them. She left the school. Her parents blamed her. She was shamed in front of her family. When she found herself left unaided, one day, she left. She went to Delhi," he continued.

"These influential guys, with the help of their families' connections, helped them to close the case. They were set free." Everyone listened to what he said.

"In the end, money wins over the truth," Virat narrated.

"And you know sir, who this girl was? Who were these guys? They were the sons of the so-called reputed entrepreneurs: Singhal's son, Gowerker's son and Turex's son. All those families you people tag as innocent." Virat declared.

"And you killed them? Don't you have faith in the law of this country?" one of the judges asked.

"Ideally, you should believe in the law of your country. A criminal can never go without being arrested, however cunning or influential he may be. For any crime, there is always a punishment," a judge tried to advise the teenage boy who had now no belief left in the system.

"They may not have suffered a lot if your law would have done its work in the right manner, but here, in this case, it was the girl who suffered, who became the victim. That one incident changed her whole life, shattered it into pieces just because she was at fault of loving a person who was a crook. She had let them go and her father remained mute. At such a young age, she had seen so many ups and downs in her life, but after listening to her pain, I could not resist to go on my own to take this bold step and take revenge on her behalf. But I think the time has now come when you should all know the truth. This way, at least some justice is done to this girl," Virat said.

"Who was that girl?" Mr Devang asked as this was a new angle of the case, unexplored.

"That girl was Mahi." Everyone was quiet in the court.

The judge listened carefully and thought for a while. "How are you so sure? There is a law and order in this country and you by yourself went to take revenge. You turned yourself into a psychopath," he said looking at him

"You are right, sir. I may have turned into a psychopath, but this girl is now everything to me. She will now rest in peace once she will come to know I fought for her." A tear rolled down his cheek and he looked at his father.

"Yes, I punished all these families for the heinous crime they committed all those years back, from raping a girl to bribing all those officers to manipulate that case," Virat confessed.

"Do you realize how many people you killed? And at what cost? You ruined all those families and killed each and every member of those families?" A judge tried to awaken his conscience. "Killing someone is not the right way. You committed bigger sins when you took all those lives."

"He needs to be punished for all of this, and better late than never." One of the judges from the panel gave his statement.

"You are right. I have full faith on your judgement and I just hope he gets a harsh punishment," the government lawyer put stressed on his crime.

"And sir, before you say something on this case, I would like to add something more to it and this story," the government lawyer gave a new angle to the case.

"Proceed," the judge gave him permission.

"Well, the girl he is talking about is dead." There was silence in court as the lawyer revealed this.

"She committed suicide a few years ago and if we examine the story Mr Virat just narrated chronologically, then he may have a lack of knowledge or is living in a self-made dream," he added.

"She is my love, do you get that? And if you say a word more…" Virat said aloud and banged his fist.

"I have something to prove what I said," the lawyer said smiling.

"To the esteemed jury members, here I want to present these papers which the opposition has also cross-checked and to the court that the girl which Mr Virat is mentioning is dead. It was an investigated case of suicide," he added handing over the paperwork of the case to the court.

"Court is adjourned for the next half an hour and today we will have a second session of this case after the lunch break while our panel examines the papers submitted to us by the lawyer." Virat was sent back to judicial custody again.

"After listening to everything we have to conclude this case, so by the next hearing, which will be the 24th hearing of the court, we will be giving our decision on this case. The court is adjourned until next week."

It was now affirmed that Virat was the culprit and would be sentenced in the next hearing.

Trial day 24: Judgment Day

And the day came for the final trial of the case. News channel reporters were sent outside the court and everyone was keen to hear the most awaited judgment.

Breaking news flashed over the TV screens: *Today's Judgment; will it be a historical judgment?*

Few people from nearby places came to the court premises with hoardings in their hands and pamphlets about how Virat should be punished cruelly and should not be given any chance to escape.

And the court started with the judgment.

There was pin drop silence in the premises and only a few voices from the people shouting and protesting outside could be heard.

"Whatever he has done is wrong in every sense," the judge said. "What hurt me more is that you took the law into your own hands," he added. "You will not be hanged but will be imprisoned, but before that do you wish to say anything?" the judge said, proceeding.

"I thought this educated society is well behaved and we have good people around, but I was wrong. They are all a part of the same society who worship rapists and kills the victim. We feel that a girl's character is lost when she is raped. But it's not true… Character comes from the inner soul and it remains clean always," Virat stopped in between. He looked at his father; he had become weaker. His father looked as if he could finally sleep after many days. His hair was white and the wrinkles were easily noticeable on his face which were more prominent because of the stress.

"We are not going to be too harsh to this person and since our law has a few flaws that the victims who are underage and not adults can be given no strict punishment. We can either send him to jail or to a rehabilitation centre. We discussed this at length with the other esteemed dignitaries in the committee. Concluding what our esteemed panel thinks, and here I thank Mr S.K. Verma for giving me this opportunity to give the most awaited judgment of the decade. This is how we can help our new generation. Mr Virat will be sent to the rehabilitation centre, where he will serve society and will have to prove that he will actually change in these seven years and only then will he be released under the observation of an NGO." Everyone applauded to the judgment.

"And we hereby will draft a new era over such cases and a bill with stricter punishments will be passed in the Parliament." The court was dismissed. Virat's father hugged him hard before he was sent to the rehabilitation centre.

Three months later...

In the cell, there was a guy sitting in a croquet posture, putting his head over his knees, thinking about his future. The cell where he was kept was dark; there was no natural light. This guy was Virat who had now settled in his new world where he was alone. He did not want to make friends; nor did he want to forget what had happened to him in all these months. He could not believe that Mahi was dead, and if she was, then who was that girl he had met at Lajpat Nagar! He had millions of questions in his mind, but no one to share them with. Other inmates in the different cells were asleep. It was six in the evening and suddenly a warden came near the cell and unlocked it.

"There is a phone call for you, you have just two minutes." Virat stood up, followed him and went towards the room where the phone was kept.

He picked up the speaker and said, "Hello, who's this?"

"Mahi…" Virat heard a soft voice from the other side.

Recommended Reading

When Karma Goes Upside Down

Dishant Huria

By day, Aarush is struggling to get admission in a reputed college; by night, he is a technical support man working in a call centre. His lady love plans the most unexpected surprise gift on their fourth love-anniversary – a break-up! In trying to accept that she is gone, he bumps into several girls and an older woman who fascinates him no end.

Join Aarush as he tries to find a way into love and happiness *When Karma Goes Upside Down.*

Dishant Huria has been a reluctant journalist and an active blogger. A sports and travel enthusiast, he is a part of a digital marketing firm.

ISBN: 9789382665922; Pages: 200; MRP: 195/-; Binding: Paperback

---

37 + Grace Marks
Vishal Anand

Viraj falls head over heels in love with his classmate Nimisha, who could make boys on campus go crazy. While his friends Punit and Sahil just want to have fun, Viraj wants more from his life and love.

Life has led Viraj to the edge of a cliff. He has a choice to make – to forget everything and jump, or fight.

Welcome to *37 + Grace Marks*, Viraj's journey to discover that there is more to life than marks.

Vishal Anand holds a Master's degree in Business Economics and works with a talent consulting partner to several domestic and international companies in Bangalore.

ISBN: 9789382665977; Pages: 200; MRP: 175/-; Binding: Paperback

Wottaplot!
Santosh Vishwanath

Raj sets out to conquer a piece of land around the Bangalore city. Through some humorous and some hopeless misadventures, he realizes that it isn't as easy as it sounded.

While the earlier trigger was to prove a point to someone else, it slowly dawns upon him that he needs to prove things to himself first.

Wottaplot! is the story of an average Bangalorean's plight to own a small piece of land and the adventures that follow.

Santosh makes a living by making sense out of numbers and at the same time, loves to live in a world of words. A true Bangalorean himself, he is fond of telling stories.

ISBN: 9789382665939; Pages: 208; MRP: 195/-; Binding: Paperback

---

Inside the Heart of Hope
Rishabh Puri

Rick has a medical condition that makes his life different from the rest. But he sees this as an opportunity to cherish life and all the bitter-sweet gifts it brings with it.

Amidst frequent visits to the doctor, multiple surgeries that risk his life being, and a life that meant surveillance all the time, Rick falls in love.

Inside the Heart of Hope is a story of strong will, perseverance and optimism which will make you wonder if sky is really the limit.

Rishabh Puri loves to meet new people and explore the world. He enjoys sitcoms and movies, likes to read and experiment in the kitchen.

ISBN: 9789382665960; Pages: 136; MRP: 150/-; Binding: Paperback

Twenty Twenty: A Race Against Time
Anuraag Srivastava

Abhi and Aditi are siblings who want to realise their dreams in the big city. In the midst of all the struggle and success, if they are not able to resolve a crisis in twenty days, their very existence can come under threat. In short, they have to hit sixes on every bouncer thrown at them.

Twenty Twenty is a story of betrayal, deceit and relationships, where a master planner devises games, to get to his own ambitions.

Anuraag Srivastava has been a banker for over eighteen years now. Presently based at Ghaziabad, he is a poet, guitarist, photographer and avid reader.

ISBN: 9789382665915; Pages: 224; MRP: 195/-; Binding: Paperback

---

Messed Up! But All For Love
Arvind Parashar

Neil and Gauri are deeply in love, but Neil's fitness consultant Srinya seems to be stirring some trouble in their lives. Drishti is a TV news anchor and journalist and her husband Somesh, a top cop. They bump into Neil and his friends in Cuba and things change.

The havoc ensues when Drishti gets abducted and Neil is framed for it.

In short, their lives are *Messed Up! But All for Love*.

Arvind Parashar has been a corporate leader in firms like GE, Dell and Genpact. He is a painter who enjoys road trips and gives motivational lectures across leading educational institutes.

ISBN: 9789382665946; Pages: 176; MRP: 175/-; Binding: Paperback

www.ingramcontent.com/pod-product-compliance
Lightning Source LLC
Chambersburg PA
CBHW060120260626
47160CB00005B/1949